Murder at
Redwood Cove

MURDER AT REDWOOD COVE

Janet Finsilver

LYRICAL UNDERGROUND
Kensington Publishing Corp.
www.kensingtonbooks.com

LYRICAL UNDERGROUND BOOKS are published by

Kensington Publishing Corp.
119 West 40th Street
New York, NY 10018

All Kensington titles, imprints, and distributed lines are available at special quantity discounts for bulk purchases for sales promotion, premiums, fund-raising, educational, or institutional use.

Special book excerpts or customized printings can also be created to fit specific needs. For details, write or phone the office of the Kensington Sales Manager: Kensington Publishing Corp., 119 West 40th Street, New York, NY 10018. Attn. Sales Department. Phone: 1-800-221-2647.

Lyrical Press logo Reg. U.S. Pat. & TM Off.

First Electronic Edition: October 2015
eISBN-13: 978-1-61650-929-3
eISBN-10: 1-61650-929-5

First Print Edition: October 2015
ISBN-13: 978-1-61650-930-9
ISBN-10: 1-61650-930-9

Printed in the United States of America

To my husband, E.J., for all of his support and encouragement.

ACKNOWLEDGMENTS

I'm very lucky to have many wonderful people in my life. My husband, E.J., encouraged me to follow my dream and write a mystery. I am forever grateful. The book was reviewed by two critique groups. The writers who shared their sage advice are the following: Colleen Casey, Michael Cooper, Margaret Dumas, Claire Johnson, Rena Leith, Staci McLaughlin, Ann Parker, Carole Price, Penny Warner, and Gordon Yano.

A thank you to Karen Hattori and Lann Westbrook for reading the book and giving me their feedback and to Georgia Drake for her ideas and support. I received very helpful information from Dennis McKiver from his years of service with the California Department of Fish and Game; Don Miller, retired Lieutenant, Mendocino County Sheriff's Office; and Mary Miller, retired Sergeant, Fort Bragg Police Department.

A special thank you to my agent, Dawn Dowdle, and my editor, John Scognamiglio. These are two of the most on top of it people I've ever known, and I have the good fortune to be working with them. Thank you all.

Chapter 1

What a horrible way to die—falling forty feet and landing on jagged rocks in the swirling ocean. I couldn't stop thinking about what my boss had told me, even as I forced my attention back to the present. My nails dug into the armrests as the small plane tilted to the side.

My thoughts slid away again. How did the accident happen? Had the inn's manager, the man I was replacing, slipped and fallen on a rugged edge? Had a piece of the treacherous cliff crumbled beneath him?

My fingers traced the embossed company emblem in the stiff brown leather briefcase resting on the seat next to me. When my employer, Michael Corrigan, called and instructed me to get to the bed-and-breakfast as quickly as possible, I felt a surge of excitement mixed with anxiety. It was my first assignment as an executive administrator for Resorts International. A rush of fear followed. It was also my fourth job in three years, not counting my work on the family ranch. Would this one be the fit I had failed to find? Was there even a niche out there for me?

The aircraft dipped and bucked its way through one air pocket after another. I gripped the armrests tighter, stomach lurching with each bump, and resisted the temptation to squeeze my eyes shut. The aircraft lined up with a toothpick-sized landing strip cut out of a thick stand of trees. Lower . . . lower . . . the wheels bumped, and the plane swerved from side to side. Off in the distance, the small patch of dirt runway ended abruptly at a cliff's edge. Only open ocean beyond.

The pilot steadied the wheel, and the plane's path straightened out. I let go of the seat and uncurled my stiff fingers.

He turned. "Welcome to Mendocino County."

I took a deep breath. "Thanks for getting me here on such short notice."

The pilot taxied the plane toward a black Mercedes. "Most people wouldn't thank me after going through all that turbulence." He chuckled.

"My family has a resort in Wyoming with backcountry lodges we fly into. I never learned to like rides like this, but I got used to them."

I zipped up my down jacket, glad I'd left it on for the chilly flight. The plane stopped, and I unbuckled the seat belt, stood, and pulled my tan cowboy hat down by the chin strap from the overhead bin, the braided horsehair coarse to the touch. I stared at the parting gift from my family and then looked at the portfolio. The known and loved in one hand and the new in the other.

The pilot finished adjusting his controls, got up, opened the door, and unlatched the steps.

"Thanks again."

"Michael is a good friend of mine. When he called and asked if I could fly you in from Santa Rosa, I was happy to help."

I slung the briefcase over my shoulder and held my hat by the brim. I stepped out and grabbed on to the railing to descend the narrow ladder. A blast of cold ocean air whipped my hair around my face, stinging my cheeks. I touched solid ground with one foot, then the other, and breathed a sigh of relief.

The pilot followed me down and pulled my luggage from the cargo area.

A long pencil of a man approached, tugging at a sleeve of his black jacket. "Hi. I'm Daniel Stevens, from Redwood Cove Bed-and-Breakfast."

I extended my hand. "Kelly Jackson, executive administrator with Resorts International."

We shook hands, and he reached for my carry-on and duffel bag and turned to the car. A sleek black ponytail swung across his back. The high cheekbones and almond-colored skin hinted at Native American ancestry.

He put the bags down and started to open the front passenger door for me. Hesitating, he reached for the door to the backseat instead.

"Front seat is fine," I assured him. "Better view."

He opened the front door. "I'll load your things, and we'll be off."

The wind picked up, and he buttoned the bottom two buttons of his jacket over his starched white shirt. He ran his finger around the stiff collar.

I settled into the passenger seat, put the briefcase on the floor, and placed my hat on top of it. Looking out at the ocean, I noticed a wall of fog hunkered down on the horizon.

Daniel got in. "Sorry about the mix-up with the doors"—he started the car—"I haven't picked up guests before. I don't know the protocol."

"No problem."

His shoulders dropped a fraction of an inch.

I leaned back into the leather. Right. Bob Phillips would've picked me up. But he was dead.

"How is Mr. Phillips's wife doing? I understand she suffered a heart attack."

"She's in Santa Rosita Hospital in intensive care. Her kids are with her."

We slowly drove off the gravel road and pulled onto California's Coastal Highway One.

"They'd been married thirty-two years," Daniel said.

Thirty-two years. A lifetime. My marriage had lasted four. I couldn't imagine the depth of the woman's loss. A piece of her life had vanished.

Even in early afternoon, the tall redwood border heavily shadowed the road. Glimpses of blue water flickered through the trees. I pulled myself out of my contemplation of the scenery and back to the work I had to do.

"Daniel, I'd like to go to the site of the accident first. The company wants me to send a report and see if there's anything that suggests we should add some new warning information in our guest booklets."

"No problem. It's pretty much on our way."

"The company job description says you're a maintenance supervisor. I'd like to know more about what you do."

He smiled for the first time. "That's a fancy title for handyman and jack-of-all-trades. My usual uniform is a denim shirt and jeans." He turned off the highway, following a sign directing them to Redwood Cove. "The B&B is a historic mansion. Upkeep is ongoing. I do some of the work and schedule what needs to be done by specialists. Recently Bob had me helping with the books and payments."

"Thanks for the information. I'll be managing the property until someone else can be hired. I'm sure I'll have some questions for you."

We drove through a couple of short town blocks filled with nineteenth-century New England–style architecture and then out onto a wide, open area of grass and bluffs overlooking the Pacific Ocean.

"These are the headlands." He parked in an empty lot. "Bob walked here often. It's public parkland."

Daniel led the way along a dirt path that meandered near the cliff's border then dropped down about ten feet below the edge. We walked out onto a flat area surrounded by ocean on three sides. He pointed to craggy, kelp-covered rocks below. "That's where he was found."

I had envisioned a trail close to the rim that might have collapsed or a place where people heard the siren call of a better view and stepped too far out. But a few people could comfortably picnic at this site, and the view was pretty much the same from wherever you looked out on the small plateau.

I frowned. "Do they know what happened?"

"Not sure. The police are doing an autopsy. Checking to see if he had a stroke or a heart attack." He looked at his feet and then to the froth-capped waves below.

"Is there anything else?" I prodded gently.

A momentary pause. "No." Daniel turned, and his long legs took him quickly to the top of the bluff. I joined him. We stopped and gazed down one more time.

"No, get back!" The wind snatched the shrill scream of a child. "Get back! Get back!"

A small boy rode his bike in our direction, struggling to stay upright on the sandy path. A stubby-legged dog worked to keep up, huge ears flapping in the wind. The bike began to topple. He jumped off, dropped it, and ran toward us, waving two slim arms above his head, shouting. The baying dog next to him had more luck being heard.

The boy stumbled and crashed face-first into tall grass next to the trail. We both ran to him. Daniel reached him just as the boy sat up, terrified eyes glued on the slender man. Tears streamed down his cheeks.

My heart wrenched at the anguish on the boy's face.

Daniel knelt beside him. "Tommy, are you hurt?"

A slight shake of his head from side to side. The boy began taking in gulps of air, faster and faster. Then deep sobs started.

Daniel put his arms around him and held him close.

"It's my fault," the boy struggled to speak. "It's my fault he's dead." His small fist struck Daniel's starched white shirt, leaving a brown smudge. "It's my fault."

Chapter 2

Another hit. The dog poked his large head into the boy's side. Daniel held him closer.

The boy sank into the man's chest, burying his face. His slender shoulders heaved as the sobs continued. "He's dead. Uncle Bob's dead."

A soul-grabbing sound like nothing I'd ever heard filled the air. The hound's head was thrown back, nose pointed to the sky, ears dangling down his back, as he howled a chilling, baritone cry.

"Quiet," Daniel said sternly.

The dog's head came down, and his muzzle snapped shut.

Souls were saved.

The boy unfolded slowly out of Daniel's arms, stood, and wiped his eyes on the arm of his gray sweatshirt, leaving wet blotches on the sleeve.

"Are you okay?" I stepped toward him.

He nodded in reply but didn't say a word.

"I'm Ms. Jackson." I leaned down and put my hand out. "What's your name?" He appeared about ten.

I received a tentative, small hand in return and gently shook it.

Puffy red eyes looked at me. "Tommy," came the barely audible whisper.

"Nice to meet you." I looked at the canine that was seriously studying me. "What's your dog's name?"

"Fred."

The dog's lips pulled back in a grin at the mention of his name. His small tank of a body wiggled from one end to the other as he gazed at the boy.

"Come on. Time to get you home." Daniel stood and ruffled Tommy's light blond hair. He turned to me. "His mom works at the inn, and they live on site."

I walked to the bike and picked it up.

"I can get that." Daniel reached for it.

"I'm fine. You have two charges to take care of."

The tricolored dog lumbered beside us as we walked up the trail, Daniel's hand resting on Tommy's shoulder. A gust of wind sent a faint mist from the ocean over us, the salty tang filling my nostrils.

What on earth had the boy meant when he said it was his fault Bob Phillips was dead? I was dying to ask the question, but I knew now wasn't the time.

Daniel pulled keys from his pocket as we approached the car and aimed one at the trunk. By the time we reached it, the lid was up. He placed the bike in the back and put rags under the protruding front wheel. I spied a couple of blankets. "You're well supplied." I grabbed them and covered part of the backseat to protect it from Fred's dogginess.

"This is country living up here. You go prepared." He tied the lid down with rope. "Tommy, you and Fred hop in the back."

The boy climbed in. Daniel reached down to help the short-legged animal maneuver onto the car seat. Fred gave Tommy a quick lick and leaned against him.

We drove from the headlands to Redwood Cove Bed-and-Breakfast in less than ten minutes. Daniel turned the Mercedes into a narrow driveway. A two-story white clapboard house and a riot of periwinkle blue, fuchsia, and deep gold among massive amounts of green vegetation came into view. Bursts of white flowers climbed upward on a lush vine. Every eave dripped ornate curls of gingerbread trim. A well-dressed Victorian lady.

Passing the guest parking, we pulled into a loading area at the back of the house and parked next to a red Toyota pickup with RED-WOOD COVE BED-AND-BREAKFAST painted on the side.

Daniel opened the rear door. "Out you come." He helped Fred make the descent. Tommy jumped out after him and ran for the house.

He took the porch stairs two at a time. He stopped at the back door, his hand on the knob, and glanced back. "Thank you, Daniel." His pale face turned to me. "Nice to meet you, Ms. Jackson." He opened the door, held it for Fred, and rushed inside.

Grabbing my hat and briefcase, I stepped out, took a welcome stretch, and sighed. A red-eye flight from Cheyenne, small planes in between, and hours of missed sleep hit me like a two-by-four.

Daniel smiled. "I'll get your bags and meet you inside. We can fix you tea or coffee, if you'd like."

"Coffee would be great. Thanks." I walked up the wooden stairs, following the boy's path. I entered a warm, embracing work area and kitchen combined and almost swooned as the aroma of baking cookies enveloped me. Right. Food. Hours ago there had been a rubbery-egg airport breakfast.

Two women looked up from a large table covered with neatly stacked piles of paper. A young blonde approached, an almost visible energy field surrounding her. "I'm Suzie Ward, manager of Ralston Hotel. Our place is just down the road." The enthusiastic hand I shook gave me a spark of energy.

"Kelly Jackson, Resorts International."

The other woman, large-framed and gaunt, slowly rose and walked around the table. "I'm Helen Rogers." She extended her hand. It was limp, as if unable to hold its own weight.

The spark extinguished, and my shoulders sagged.

"I came over to help Helen." Suzie looked away. "Bob's death has been difficult. The community lost one of its finest members."

"I'm sorry." I wished I had comforting words to ease the pain, but no magic vocabulary materialized.

"I see Tommy came home with you. I'm his mom, and I'm an assistant here." Helen ran her fingers through short, wavy brown hair interlaced with gray. "I'm so glad to have you here." Dark hollows beneath her eyes hinted at sleepless nights.

Daniel entered. "I'll put your bags in your room."

"I'll go with you. It's been a long day, and I want to freshen up." I looked at the women. "I'll be taking over Bob's duties until his position is filled. I'll be back shortly. I'd appreciate it if you'd catch me up on what's happening." The corners of my mouth managed a slight upward curve, defying the gravity of tiredness. "It's nice meeting you."

I followed Daniel down a narrow, wood-floored hallway. He paused as he started to turn left and pointed to a door on our right. "That's our conference room. Extra linens are in the closet next to it."

The hall had long, rectangular windows framing a lush backyard. We headed toward a door at the end of the hallway. Daniel unlocked it, and we stepped into a large, bright room. He deposited my bags on the floor.

A studio apartment–sized beige couch occupied the right side with a large oak cabinet directly ahead. An open door in the far corner revealed the edge of a bed. However, what demanded my attention was the part of the room that pushed out into a small strip of garden and pulled in the ocean beyond. Almost at cliff's edge—glass roof, glass to the floor.

"Wow!"

"Yeah, it's pretty spectacular." He stared with me for a moment. "We have a lot of foggy days here. Light's at a premium."

A small table with four chairs, window seats, and a beckoning recliner completed the furnishings. I spied a wood-burning stove against the wall near the sunroom. I put my things on the couch, took off my jacket, and tossed it on top of them.

"This is a self-contained unit." He led me to a galley-like area. "There's a small fridge stocked with a variety of food choices. Nothing fancy, but handy for late nights or long afternoons." A two-burner stove with a microwave above it provided the basic preparation equipment. And then there was the gleaming coffeemaker.

I laughed. "A sailboat kitchen that has a commercial-grade coffee machine with all the bells and whistles." My big, burly boss, Michael Corrigan, owner of Resorts International, prized a quality cup of coffee. A note on the glistening giant said fresh beans were in the canisters.

"Priorities. What can I say?" Daniel grinned. He walked back into the main room, opened a cabinet, and slid out a state-of-the-art computer. "There are file folders here"—he pulled out a drawer—"and office supplies are in that one." He pointed to the other side. "Your company does it right."

"Yes, it does." I looked around and then turned back to him. "Daniel, it's been a pleasure to meet you. Thank you for all your help."

"Sure thing."

"I'm sorry about Bob Phillips. It must be hard on everyone."

"It is. He was a great guy."

We looked at each other for a moment. Strangers sharing a moment of sadness.

"Let me know if you need anything." He grabbed a card out of his pocket. "This has my cell phone number. Works in town, but it's spotty in the surrounding area." He scribbled on it. "Here's my home phone, as well."

"Thanks."

He handed it to me.

"The keys to the company pickup are on a hook next to the back door. The Mercedes stays at the airport. It's used by company execs when they fly in and for picking up guests. I'm going to take it up there now and swap it for my van."

A light tapping at the door interrupted us.

I opened it. A large basket was shoved up at me.

"Welcome to Redwood Cove Bed-and-Breakfast," Tommy said from beneath it.

I took it and admired the colorful collection of welcoming gifts. "This is wonderful." The fruit consisted of strawberries, bananas, and apples. The chocolate wrapper said REDWOOD COVE CHOCOLATE COMPANY, and the reading material included a newspaper, the *Redwood Cove Beacon,* and the *Mendocino County Visitors' Guide.*

"Thank you."

"You're welcome." Tommy was gone.

Daniel said, "He's a neat kid, but he's having a tough time . . . in a lot of ways."

"What did he mean it was his fault Bob died?"

He sighed and shook his head. "Ten-year-old logic, or lack of it." Daniel leaned against the wall. "He was supposed to work with Bob on his fifth-grade science project after school the day Bob died. Tommy got in trouble and had to stay after. He figures if he'd gotten home on time, Bob wouldn't have gone for a walk and fallen off the cliff."

"I'm sure people have told him it wasn't his fault."

"Oh yeah. Many times. His decision's set like cement." Another sigh. "You can jackhammer concrete and haul it away, but we haven't found the solution for Tommy's guilt."

"The fact they were related must make it even harder."

"They weren't. Bob had taken Tommy under his wing. Said he'd be an uncle for him. They did things together like an uncle and a nephew would."

"I appreciate your sharing that with me." I shuddered to think of the burden the child carried.

"Is there anything else I can get for you?"

"I'm fine, and again, thanks."

Daniel closed the door. I sank down on the couch and leaned back into a mound of down cushions. The room looked out across an inlet to a craggy rock face covered with various shades of green. Endless ocean, almost unbearable to look at with the brightly reflected sun glazing the surface, was off to the right. Three gulls floated past the window on an air current, their wings still. It was as if I could reach out and touch them.

The calm moment was pure bliss, but it was time to move. My first solo assignment with the company. Growing up in the resort business was one thing. Being in charge was another. As I stepped into a dead man's shoes, I asked myself whether I could do it. It wasn't only my boss counting on me—employees and guests expected me to keep things running until they found a replacement for Bob.

"Get up, weary body." I rolled off the couch, explored the small refrigerator, and grabbed a miniature bottle of Pellegrino. A mirror hung on the sitting room wall. A quick check showed I was becoming an Orphan Annie look-alike as my hair reacted to the moist air. My jeans and black turtleneck had survived the flight just fine. I appreciated the company's casual dress policy. Suits and heels didn't work for me, as I had learned from Job Number Two.

Unpacking the duffel bag and carry-on didn't take long. I put on a light blue fleece vest, pulled my fanny pack out of the briefcase, and stepped into the hallway.

"Deputy Sheriff, you're not listening," growled a raspy male voice from the nearby conference room.

"Ivan, there's nothing to go on."

"There could be. Investigate!" the angry voice demanded.

"Investigate what? Tell me one thing I could check into."

"It was murder, and you know it!"

Chapter 3

Startled, I glanced out a partly open hall window. A female guest sat up in a lounge chair and looked uneasily over her shoulder. The woman frowned, gathered up her blanket and book, and disappeared around a path at the edge of the house. I headed toward the sound of the voices. The word *murder* didn't bode well for a smooth beginning to my job.

The meeting room door was slightly ajar. I pushed it open, glanced around, and thought to myself it could have been your everyday senior citizens' meeting, except the subject appeared to be murder and there was a police officer in the room. The monochromatic hair color of the participants ranged from salt-and-pepper to ethereal silver.

"I know no such thing," said a stout gentleman in a tan uniform with a MENDOCINO COUNTY DEPUTY SHERIFF's emblem sewn on his sleeve.

A towering man slammed his ham-sized fist on the table. "It's not right. Something has to be done."

The sound of the smacking hand sent a jolt through me.

The man looked up and froze.

"Sorry to interrupt. I'm Kelly Jackson, executive administrator for Resorts International, the owner of this property. I'm here as acting manager and wanted to introduce myself." And rein your group in. Loud discussions about murder didn't partner well with a B&B vacation. I stepped in and closed the conference room door.

"I am Rudy Doblinsky." A man seated to the right of the table pounder stood, approached me, and reached out his hand.

I extended mine, expecting the usual handshake. The man gently took it, turned it palm down, bowed with his arm behind his back, and kissed my hand, all in one flowing motion.

He released my hand and nodded his head toward the man who had been shouting. "And this is my brother, Ivan."

Ivan's massive shoulders, pockmarked cheeks, full mustache, and shaggy mane of hair reminded me of an old, battle-scarred bull walrus. The family traits showed in Rudy's face, but he was much smaller than his brother, had a neatly trimmed beard and a quiet air about him.

The officer stood, shoved his chair back, and held out his hand. "Deputy Sheriff Bill Stanton."

I shook his hand. "Glad to meet you."

My gaze settled on the last person in the room, a dapper, diminutive man attired in a diamond-patterned wool vest, white shirt, and gray bow tie.

He gave a little wave. "I'm Herbert Winthrop. However, we dispensed with that name a while back, and people usually call me the Professor." He pulled out a chair. "We heard you were coming. Please join us. We were friends of Bob, and we're discussing what happened to him." He gave a slight smile. "Considering your position, I suspect you'd like to know about our concerns."

I sat between him and the officer. "Since I'll be managing the property for a while, I appreciate being kept in the loop."

Ivan dropped his large bulk into a chair that groaned a protest. He looked at Deputy Sheriff Stanton. "What about the break-in last night?" Ivan boomed. "That must mean something."

"Ivan, don't even go there with me." Stanton shook his head and tapped a couple of photographs on the table. "You were the one at the town hall meeting who pointed out home robberies often occur when someone dies or has been taken to the hospital, and you asked us to do more patrols in those situations." He perused the photos and then pushed them over to me. "There's nothing to suggest what happened last night isn't just that."

I picked them up. "Where were these pictures taken?"

"Bob Phillips's house. Thanks to these two," the deputy said grudgingly, "the thieves didn't get anything. Rudy called the robbery in, and a deputy was nearby."

The time was night; the brightness of the photo was like day. One picture showed a license plate attached to the back of a silver Toyota, numbers easily readable. The other captured a wide-eyed young Caucasian man wearing a dark watch cap, dreadlocks falling to his shoulders. Another man had his denim-covered back to the camera, a side profile of his face showing. They were carrying a large-screen television between them.

"And another thing," the officer added. "Guys like these usually have a twelve-gauge handy. They can do a lot of damage, fast."

"Ivan has, what you call it, a lead foot?" Rudy grinned. "Poof. We were gone." He studied his hands. "We promised Bob's kids we'd watch over the house."

"I know you want to help, but you two need to be careful. You hear me?" The deputy looked at them with a mixture of fondness and frustration.

I put the photos on the table.

Deputy Sheriff Stanton glanced at them. "By the way, what in the world did you use for light? It must've scared the bejesus out of those guys."

"I borrow the searchlight from *Nadia*." Ivan couldn't have whispered if he tried. "She's not going fishing for a while, so I put to good use."

"I thought you retired that old boat," Stanton said.

Ivan began to puff up. "Old boat? My *Nadia*?"

The Professor rapped the table with his pen. "Back to the point at hand." He looked at the officer. "Will you do anything further to investigate Bob's death?"

"I'll read the autopsy report. If there's something unusual there, I'll act on it."

"Was there anything Bob was working on that might have gotten him into trouble?" The Professor turned to me. "Bob was an ardent conservationist."

"After your call questioning his death, I checked with Fran at Fish and Game. He was trying to get an area of the beach protected for the snowy plover. Some of the locals objected to that." He shook his head. "But murder, no." He looked around the group. "There's the abalone poaching your group has helped with, and the marijuana busts, but that's not new."

Poaching? Drugs? Wasn't Redwood Cove the primo tourist destination for northern California? How were these people involved? Had Bob been murdered? I had a lot of questions that needed answers. "Other than the robbery, why do you think he was murdered?"

"He knew the cliffs like the back of his hand," the Professor said.

"He walked them almost every day, and he was always careful. Where he fell didn't have any hidden dangers."

I agreed about the location based on my observations.

"And he had a physical two weeks ago," Rudy said. "The doctor gave him an excellent report."

Deputy Sheriff Stanton stood. "Gotta go, folks. If you find something concrete I can work with, I'll check it out." The deputy shook his head. "But I think it was just a tragic accident. I know it's hard to accept that's what happened."

He pulled a card from his pocket and handed it to me. "It was nice meeting you, Ms. Jackson. If I can be of any assistance, please don't hesitate to call."

"Thanks, Deputy Sheriff Stanton. It was a pleasure to meet you."

The officer left, and the Professor turned to me.

"Ms. Jackson, we had an idea when we heard you were coming." The Professor smiled benignly at me. "We thought it might be helpful to reconstruct the day of Bob's death." Again the engaging smile. "Our group imagined you'd like to get up to speed with what he was doing as quickly as possible."

The door burst open. "I'm so sorry to be late. The brownies seemed to take forever." A plump woman rushed in holding a plate heaped with bars oozing chocolate. Smile lines permanently etched her cheeks. The sweet scent of perfume trailed in behind her. She placed the dish on the table and looked at me. "I'm Mary Rutledge," emitted a soft, breathless voice as she seated herself at the table.

A munchkin-sized woman followed Mary, her cane tapping a rhythmic beat. "Gertrude Plumber." Her wizened face peered at me intently. "And that's the last time Gertrude is to be mentioned. Call me Gertie." She settled next to Mary.

"Pleased to meet you. Kelly Jackson, the temporary manager here."

"Deputy Stanton isn't planning to do an investigation unless something new comes to light," the Professor told the newcomers. "We were just beginning to talk with Ms. Jackson about gathering information."

"Bob had one of those gadgets your company uses." Gertie looked around the group. "A Blackbush? Was that it?"

"A BlackBerry, my dear." The Professor smiled at her.

"He was forever making notes on the infernal thing. Maybe you could find something there," Gertie said.

I nodded. All managers used the same system for calendaring appointments and checking e-mail.

Ivan grinned, or at least I thought that was what all the teeth represented. If it wasn't a grin, I should probably run. His teeth resembled those I imagined the wolf showed in *Little Red Riding Hood.*

"Yah. You tell us what he did," he said with a vigorous nod of his head.

"You could perhaps talk to the people he visited the day of his death and share what you discover with us." The Professor paused. "We could see if we felt anything was unusual. We've known Bob for ages."

I thought for a moment. "Your idea about finding out what he most recently did for the business is a good one. How much I can tell you depends on the nature of his conversations and what he was doing."

"Certainly, Ms. Jackson." The Professor nodded. "We appreciate any assistance you can provide."

"Please, all of you, call me Kelly."

"Bob was kind enough to let us meet here every week. He joined us whenever possible. Can our group still use the facilities?" the Professor asked.

"Yes, you're welcome to use the room. However, I believe one of the guests heard your comment about murder and was disturbed by it. The comfort of our guests comes first."

"My brother, Ivan, gets carried away. His passionate Russian roots take over at times," Rudy said. "It won't happen again."

"Sorry," rumbled Ivan. "Madam, please accept my many apologies."

"I'll make sure the door is closed." The Professor's intense blue eyes twinkled at me. "We'd love to have you meet with us."

"Thank you. I'd like to join you as work permits."

Mary's eyes peeked over the top of her gold-framed glasses. "Thank you, honey, for helping with our investigation." She pushed the platter of decadent sweets toward me. "My grandkids say these are the best. Please try one."

Grandma investigating? "Does your group have a name?"

Rudy stood and pulled his slightly crooked frame to full height. "We, madam, are the Silver Sentinels."

Chapter 4

The Professor arched an eyebrow. "It's a bit melodramatic, but we like it."

"Best undercover as long as we're not ten feet under." Ivan chuckled.

"Ivan, don't say that anymore." Gertie rapped the table again with her cane. "Enough!"

"I like it," he said.

"I don't," Gertie snapped back, "and the others don't, either. It's ghoulish."

Mary pulled a skein of yarn and needles from a voluminous bag and began knitting furiously. Eyes looked everywhere but at Ivan. The needles clacked.

"Our mortality confronts us each morning when we wake once again and with the death of friends," the Professor stated quietly. "We have some unique opportunities to do detective work, but . . . we can do without the reminder about where we'll end up."

I was intrigued. "What exactly does your group do?"

"We assist local law enforcement."

"Rudy was robbed." Mary patted him on the knee. "That's what got us started."

He nodded. "Slick pickpocket routine."

"The police said they were having a rash of similar crimes targeting tourists," the Professor volunteered.

"Yah. I fooled them. I had my go-to-lunch clothes on. The chess club meets at Rosie's Grill every two weeks." He laughed. "I only carry an ID card and some change. The café puts the meal on my monthly bill."

"We're members of a community group," Gertie said. "Rudy told them what was happening and asked if they wanted to do something. It was discussed and eventually dropped."

"Several of us talked after the meeting and wanted to pursue it further. Coffee a few times and the Silver Sentinels were born," said the Professor.

"The only unusual thing Rudy remembered was a couple of teenagers roughhousing and bumping into him." Mary's hands continued to knit as she talked.

"We decided to watch and listen and agreed to take pictures of pairs of teenagers with our cell phones." Gertie reached for her glass of water. "Thanks again, Professor, for showing us how to do that."

"The police said most incidents took place in the afternoon." Mary beamed at me. "We picked a nice day when lots of people were out, and each of us chose a different station throughout town."

"I don't know if you've had a chance to see much of Redwood Cove yet," said the Professor. "Since the main shopping part of town only entails about five square blocks, we could cover it pretty well."

"We sat for several hours and then met," Gertie said. "None of us saw anything obvious. The Professor called Deputy Stanton and asked if there had been any incidents. He reported a man walking with his wife had lost his wallet. Had the couple remembered anything? Some teenagers playing around and running into them."

"The deputy told us where it happened." Mary's needles clicked. "It was near my station. I showed my pictures to the group."

"I remember see them pass. And"—Ivan pronounced the words like a lawyer with a killer statement—"I saw them duck under a back porch."

"They took a local shortcut across my friend Sophie's backyard." Gertie's face filled with a look of affection. "We taught together for over thirty years." Her shoulders drooped. "Doesn't see or hear too well now. Lives at the front of her house. The only time someone is at the back of her place is when maintenance guys whack the weeds four times a year."

"We explained to her what had been seen and asked if it was okay to search the backyard." Mary reached for a brownie. "She was fine with it."

"I wear gloves like on television," Ivan said.

"Ivan gave us all disposable gloves he got at the market," Mary said.

"We found a box behind a pile of wood with wallets containing drivers' licenses," the Professor shared. "They were probably trying to think of a way to sell the IDs. Credit cards and money were gone."

"We called the police. With our photographs and the stash of goods, they were able to make an arrest." Rudy's voice filled with pride.

"The Silver Sentinels solved their first case." Mary paused for a moment in the creation of what appeared to be a tiny pink sweater.

The Professor leaned forward. "Since then we've helped uncover pot selling at a local gas station and abalone poaching at a nearby beach."

"When you're gray-haired and slow-moving, you often become invisible to younger people," Gertie said quietly. "We can sit for hours on a bench with no one acknowledging us."

"It's amazing what we hear." Mary put her knitting down. "It's perfect for our investigative work."

My heart went out to these caring members of the community.

Mary reached out for Rudy's hand. "Thank you and Ivan so much for helping to create the Silver Sentinels." She squeezed his hand. "I have a new purpose in life."

"We good at finding things out." Ivan expanded his chest. "We good detectives."

A clatter of canine nails on the floor heralded the arrival of Fred. He skidded around the corner and into the room, followed by Tommy.

"Fred, my fine friend." The Professor gave a welcoming pat on his leg.

The low-slung dog made the rounds grinning widely, full body wagging. He paused at Ivan and leaned on his leg, gazing at him with deep brown, soul-searching basset hound eyes.

"My good buddy." Ivan reached down and rubbed the long, silky ears.

"Mom wanted me to ask if anyone needs anything." Tommy paused. "Do you?"

"We're fine, honey," Mary said. "Let your mom know we said thanks for asking."

"Ms. Jackson"—he looked at me—"Mom wants to know if everything in your room is okay."

"It's fine, Tommy. Why don't you call me Miss Kelly. My students found that easier than Ms. Jackson."

"Okay, Miss Kelly."

"Tommy, why aren't you in school today?" questioned Gertie.

"Parent conference day. Tomorrow afternoon, too." He was gone in a flash, Fred scampering after him.

The Professor toyed with a pen and then put it down. "We want to know if Bob met with foul play."

"I understand. It makes sense to track his meetings for that day. I'll ask the deputy for the BlackBerry." I looked at the tired, wrinkled faces intensely staring at me. "I want to work with you to get resolution on Bob's death—be it accidental or . . . not." I stood. "I'll let you know as soon as I find out something." I paused at the door. "It's been a real pleasure to meet you. Bob was lucky to have a wonderful, caring group of friends."

I retraced my steps and found Suzie and Helen bent over what appeared to be catering contracts. Daniel had a large ledger in front of him.

"Hi! Did you get settled in okay?" Suzie asked.

"Yes. It's a beautiful room."

"We're reading over Bob's plans for a meeting this Friday," Helen said. "It's the final get-together for the A Taste of Chocolate and Wine Festival Committee before the event this Saturday."

"There are a large number of regular guests coming in tomorrow, who are planning to attend this weekend." Suzie shot me a meaningful look.

Repeat visitors were a valued commodity. "What can I do to help?" Part of me was itching to see what was arranged, the other part telling me to give them some time to do their work and adjust to my presence.

"We're about done putting the paperwork together. Would discussing it in an hour work?" Suzie asked.

"Perfect. I want to go to the beach, breathe some fresh ocean air, and wash away my jet lag." I turned to go. "And it'll give me a chance to start on a report for the company."

"Wait." Helen rushed to a large tray, grabbed several warm chocolate chip cookies, and put them in a plastic container. "It's a tradition. No arguing. Guests take these with them on their first visit to Redwood Cove Beach." Helen handed me the cookies.

I laughed. "I'm not going to buck tradition." I lifted the lid and sniffed. "Oh my. What a treat!"

Helen took a canvas bag off of a hook on the wall. "Here's a back-pack with a beach mat and towels. It's part of what we offer our guests." She reached into a cupboard and pulled out a plastic bag filled with bread chunks. "These are for the seagulls if you want to feed them." Helen stuffed the crumbs into the black and tan bag and handed it to me.

I packed the cookies safely away along with my fanny pack.

"Daniel said you'd like some coffee. Regular or decaf?"

"Regular, and I drink it black."

Helen poured some in a small thermos. I tucked it in the bag, and Helen gave me directions to the beach.

I descended the stairs at the back of the inn, glad to have some time to myself to think about the Silver Sentinels and their concern that Bob might have been murdered. A delivery van was parked at the bottom with MANGINI DISTRIBUTORS emblazoned on the truck's side in bright red letters. A young Asian man in jeans and a light yellow shirt rounded the corner, almost colliding with me.

"Sorry," he blurted.

"No problem."

I glimpsed a flash of perfect white teeth. My gaze riveted on his name tag.

He followed my stare. "Yeah. I know. A bit weird." He opened the back of the van. "My mom thought the guy was the best. She has a collection of all of his movies."

I was talking to Charlie Chan.

Chapter 5

"Mom wanted me to follow in the steps of the famous detective. You know, solve murders and get the bad guys." Charlie opened the back door of the van, leaned in, and pulled out a jug of water. "Not me. I'm going to be a dentist. Four-day workweek." He placed the bottle on the back porch. Another glimpse of stunningly white teeth. "Golf Wednesdays. That's for me, man."

"Do you go to college around here?"

"No. I went to San Francisco State. Finished fall semester. This company was hiring, so here I am. Earning some money and enjoying the north coast. I'm off to the University of the Pacific in August." He slung another container out and placed it next to the first one. "Private. More expensive, but worth it." He slammed the doors shut. "It was nice meeting you," said the dentist-to-be.

"Same here."

Charlie headed for the back of the inn, and I turned and walked down the driveway.

The colorful flowers that had caught my eye as we drove in now enveloped me in their sweet scent. The air carried a fragrance a perfume company could only hope to catch in a bottle. A gust of wind brought the salty sea and a brush of mist on my cheeks.

A small, hand-painted sign ahead read BEACH in blue letters and directed people to a narrow dirt path. I wound my way downward, ice plant in bright orange and deep greens on both sides of the track. A short, steep decline in the trail, a sharp turn, and I stopped. Below me waves crashed on rugged rocks, spewing foam and creating iridescent mini-rainbows. The variation of blues in the water would have been welcome on any artist's palette.

I took in a deep breath, and the raw strength of the area filled me. I trotted the remaining length of the trail to the beach.

Low tide. I strolled along the packed, glistening sand. Gnarled pieces of driftwood lay scattered about, creating nature's artwork. A gull landed near me and cocked its head inquisitively. I walked a short distance above the tide line and put my pack down.

"So, mister gull, do you think I have something for you?" I pulled out the sack Helen had given me, grabbed a handful of crumbs, and tossed them. The bird gobbled the closest piece and gulped it down. It quickly scooped up more as a second bird approached. The first bird raised its wings and cried out as if to say, "They're mine, all mine."

I reached in for more bread and looked up. The sky was suddenly swarming with gulls. Some began to land around me; others circled and screamed overhead. I flung a handful of chunks into the crowd. One bird savagely lunged at another, chasing it away. An immature gray gull moved aside as a large adult stabbed at a morsel the smaller bird had been eyeing.

Greed. Fear. Competition. All reasons to attack. And reasons to kill. Was Bob murdered? Why would a man so familiar with the area fall to his death?

I tossed a final handful of crumbs upward. Two birds in the air fought over one large piece, their beaks locked together, wings flapping furiously.

As I packed the bag away, the ever-growing group of gulls came closer, their beaks opened wide, shrieking. The Hitchcock movie *The Birds* came to mind for a split second. I stepped back uneasily, then laughed. "Off with you!" I flung my hands in the air and the group rose as one, their raucous cries filling the air.

I picked up my backpack. "Later, guys."

Searching for somewhere to sit, I spied an outcropping of rugged black rocks that hid the rest of the beach from sight. A boulder the size of a dinosaur egg nestled in the natural windbreak, baking in the sun. The perfect backrest.

I walked over and placed my backpack next to the rock, pulled out the mat and my fanny pack, and sat, letting the warmth of the rock soak into my back. A few stalwart birds remained, lurking nearby. I took a small memo pad and pen out of my pouch. I flipped the cover back and gazed at the blank paper. Murder. Was it? *Stop it, Kelly. You need to concentrate on your job right now, which is to write the report.*

Tommy rounded the corner with Fred on his heels. "Hi." The boy stumbled in the sand, waved briefly, put his head down, and continued walking.

I had to think fast. I might be able to find out more about the day Bob died and what happened at school to keep him from his meeting. "I have cookies." I reached into my pack. "Want some?"

He paused. "Are those my mom's?"

"Yes." I held one out, the top studded with chunks of chocolate.

"They're the best." He came over and started to sit in the sand.

"Here, sit on the mat." I patted a spot beside me.

He hesitated, then sat on the far edge. Fred plopped down next to him.

I handed Tommy a cookie and took one for myself. A small crumb fell, and a gull darted in.

"They're Utah's state bird." Tommy took a bite of cookie as he observed the bird. "There's a monument in Salt Lake City celebrating the miracle of the gulls. They saved the city from a plague of crickets."

One bird walked toward us, eyeing the cookie in my hand.

"They had a protected status for a while in California because their numbers were getting smaller at Mono Lake, but then their population really grew near San Francisco. They went from less than one thousand birds in 1982 to over thirty-three thousand in 2006."

I stared at the talking encyclopedia. "How do you know so much about gulls?"

"I love learning new things." He finished his cookie, wiped a smear of chocolate from his lip with the back of his hand, and looked at my pad. "What're you doing?"

"Writing a report."

"Sort of like homework, huh?"

"Yes"—I laughed—"sort of like homework."

Tommy looked out at the sea. Fred groaned contentedly as he soaked up the rays of the sun. The boy reached out and petted him, then leaned down and fiercely wrapped his arms around the dog's neck, burying his face in the smooth black and tan fur.

"I like learning, but I hate school." His voice sounded muffled. "I'm a reject like Fred."

Reject. A harsh, cruel word. I stared at my cookie. Safer to start with the dog.

"Why do you say that about Fred?"

"He was supposed to be a cancer-detecting dog, but he failed his test," Tommy mumbled.

"I vaguely remember reading something in the newspaper about dogs and their ability to detect cancer. Can you explain it to me?"

Tommy sat up. "The dog's sense of smell is like ten thousand times better than ours."

Fred's ears twitched as a couple of sand flies buzzed around him. Tommy shooed them away.

"One study showed they can detect lung cancer and melanomas at a ninety-nine percent rate of accuracy. Another one rated their success at eighty-eight percent to ninety-seven percent. The dogs are trained to signal the person when they smell something. Cody, a poodle, would sit on the person's foot. Some dogs use different signals. They can detect other cancers, too."

Okay. Very, very smart. There was something different about him. He wasn't like most ten-year-olds I knew.

Tommy rubbed the dog's ears. "Fred was in training at the clinic where my dad went when he got sick, but he never learned how to do it. Fred was going to be given to a dog group for placement." Tears began to well up. "When my dad died, they asked us if we wanted him."

My throat constricted, and I dove into my pack for Kleenex.

Quiet sobs then some sniffles.

I took a tissue for myself and offered him one. "I have one last cookie. How about splitting it?"

He slowly reached out, took the Kleenex, wiped his eyes, and blew his nose. Fred licked his hand and stared with his deep brown hound eyes at the boy. Tommy shoved the tissue in his pocket and took the half cookie.

"Why did you call yourself a reject?"

"It's what the kids call me at school." Tommy looked at the dog. "The kids hate me. They call me names, sometimes come after me. I hate school." He rose up on his knees, reached out, picked up a piece of nearby driftwood, and hurled it at the crashing waves. "Hate it."

"Why do they pick on you?"

"I like to learn, I talk to my teachers, I get good grades, I don't play sports, I don't listen to music, I'm not interested in being popular . . ." He stopped for breath.

"That's quite a list."

"Mom thought moving here would make things better." He grabbed another piece of wood, arched his back, and flung it with a vengeance. "Didn't."

I nibbled at my cookie. "Have you talked to your teachers?"

"Yeah. But the kids get me when the teachers aren't looking. It gets worse if I say something." He stood abruptly and brushed sand from his jeans. "The day Uncle Bob died, they blocked the door and kept me from getting to class on time. I got detention. If I'd been home to meet him like I was supposed to, he wouldn't have gone for a walk and fallen off the cliff." The tears surfaced again. "If I had what it takes to make the kids leave me alone, he wouldn't be dead."

"Tommy . . ."

"Gotta go. A friend is bringing her math work over for help." Tears dripped down his cheeks. He clapped his hands, and Fred jumped up. "See you later." He raced his dog down the beach and was gone in a blink.

The kid was a regular vanishing act. I shook my head. Guilt about Bob, dead father, and living a fifth-grade nightmare. Lots to deal with.

I packed up my things and headed back to the inn. If someone planned Bob's death, they would've gotten him one way or another. If Bob was murdered, it would take one huge item off Tommy's list.

Chapter 6

I walked up the path, thinking about what I had learned. Startled, I realized I'd reached the front entrance to the property. I'd been so engrossed, I wasn't aware of how far I had come. The fog had moved in, and it was getting dark and damp. Walking up the wide front porch, the beautifully carved white pillars welcomed like open arms waiting to embrace me. I opened the front door. A fire roared in a king-sized fireplace. Logs crackled and brightly burning flames danced across the wood. The yellow and orange glow warmed me and brought an inner delight as I breathed in the pleasing scent of burning oak.

Two guests nestled in a large, plush couch facing the fire. They leafed through a notebook of restaurant menus, the fire's flames reflected on their wineglasses. They wore the uniform of the area—jeans, turtlenecks, and fleece vests. They smiled at me and went back to turning pages.

A tray piled high with a wide array of cheeses and artfully arranged crackers rested on a coffee table along with several bottles of wine. A man leaned over the cheese offerings, full lips pursed, hands clasped behind his back. He released his grip, and his right arm crept out. He pulled it back quickly as if about to be bitten.

Puzzled, I walked over and asked, "May I help you?"

"Help me? Only if you know a magical way for me to lose forty pounds so I can sample both the Huntsman and the Fourme D'Ambert." He thrust a plump hand in my direction. "Andy Brown. I own The Bay restaurant in San Francisco. Cheese is one of my signature items." He looked at his protruding belly. "In more ways than one."

"Kelly Jackson, interim manager for the inn. Pleased to meet you." I shook his hand.

"Sorry to hear about Bob. He was a good man."

"I didn't have a chance to meet him, but everyone has only had great things to say."

"I supply the cheese for the inn"—Andy nodded toward the table—"and come up on a regular basis. The deliveries tie in well with my business because it gives me an opportunity to sample new wine and cheese offerings."

I surveyed the platter. The names and a brief description for each cheese, written in an artistic, flowing hand on small cards, identified the different varieties. The Huntsman sported layered Double Gloucester Cheddar and English Stilton; the blue veins of France's Fourme d'Ambert formed a complicated pattern.

He gazed at the beckoning food and sighed, a deep and mournful sound. "Doc said diet or die."

"That's pretty direct."

"He was gentler than that, but the message was clear." He inspected the tray like a jeweler surveying rare rubies. "Ah, my passion, my love . . . cheese." He folded his ample hands together, pulling them in close to his chest, like a little boy eagerly awaiting a long-sought-after treat. "So many choices. But only one can I choose." He put his palm on his forehead and shook his head from side to side, rolling his eyes. Andy reached out, picked up a cracker, and placed a small mound of the Huntsman on it. Decision made. "Divine." He savored the morsel.

I smiled. "Andy, it's been a pleasure meeting you."

"Likewise." He cast a longing glance at the table.

I entered the dimly lit kitchen and flipped on a light. Helen's head jerked up from the hand it'd been resting on. There seemed to be more wrinkles, more sadness than when I had seen her earlier. She busily began tucking stray pieces of hair back into her clip.

"Thanks for the treats and the bread for the birds." I put the backpack on the counter and began pulling out the contents. "Is there coffee made?"

"Yes, I always keep some brewed for the guests." Helen grabbed a mug and walked to the far side of the room. "Regular or decaf?"

The orange lights glowed on two coffeemakers.

"Regular."

I sipped the coffee Helen handed me. "Excellent flavor. Where do you get it?"

"A distributor in Fort Paul, One Earth Coffee Company. Organic. Helps the people of the rainforest as well as local businesses." Helen sat. "Bob tried to get as much mileage as possible from anything we used." She reached in her pocket. "Phil, our wine person, dropped off some cases for Saturday. He said he'd like to meet with you tomorrow, if possible." She handed me a business card. "He'll be staying here later in the week to help with the festival."

PHILOPOIMEN "PHIL" XANTHIS, I read on the card. Putting it away in a pocket, I settled on a stool across from her.

Helen handed me a folder labeled A TASTE OF CHOCOLATE AND WINE FESTIVAL. "Suzie had to leave. She'll call you in the morning."

"I'll review these this evening." I took another drink of the almost-black liquid. "Great cookies. I ran into Tommy on the beach, and we shared them. He told me a bit about what's been happening at school. It sounds like he's having a difficult time."

Helen got up and rinsed some dishes in the sink. "He's smart, he's small, he's different, he's new . . . he's a perfect target."

I sipped my coffee. "I taught school for a while. I'd be happy to talk with you. Maybe we can come up with some ideas to help him."

"Tommy's sometimes a little . . . off in his interaction with other kids." Helen sighed and rested her hands on the edge of the sink. "He has a mild case of Asperger's syndrome."

Now it all made sense. I had never worked with a child who had this condition, but I had learned about it in one of my education classes. Those children were often very bright but had poor social skills.

"Is he working with anyone?"

"Yes. The school district is very supportive. He really likes his counselor."

Helen grabbed a towel, wiped her hands, and sat. "When my husband died, I thought a move would be good for Tommy. A new environment."

"I'm sorry to hear about your loss. Tommy mentioned it when he was telling me about Fred."

"We knew it was coming." Her voice caught. "You're still not prepared when it happens."

"I went through it with my grandmother. I know what you mean."

"I started searching for a job. I was a stay-at-home mom with no working skills." Her hands were dry, but she continued to rub them with the towel. "I saw an ad for an inn helper with some baking experience. Cooking was something I could do. A small residence with pets allowed was included. Dogs had to have a Canine Good Citizenship certificate, which was a breeze for Fred with all of his training."

My boss loved animals and wanted families to have pets whenever possible.

"It seemed a perfect fit. Prepare continental breakfasts, bake pastries, organize the evening wine and cheese, put together backpacks for beach trips, and a few other things."

I nodded, letting Helen know I was with her.

"I thought Redwood Cove would be perfect—the outdoors, the beach." She sighed—a soft sound whispering of pain and loss. "It hasn't worked out for him like I hoped. It's a small school, and most of the kids have known each other for a long time. He's an outsider."

"It's unfortunate it's been so hard. Tommy's a great kid."

The corners of her mouth turned up in an almost imperceptible smile. "He's a wonderful kid," she said softly. Then she shook her head. "Bob's death really dealt him a blow. They'd become close. I don't know what to do to help him."

Her hands, now quiet, rested one on top of the other on the table, the towel next to them.

I reached out and touched her arm. "I'll think about it. Let's talk some more later. Perhaps I can help."

"Thanks."

I leaned back. "I'm here to keep things running smoothly. Are there any concerns you have?"

"Not really. Daniel and Suzie have been very helpful. I do have a few questions about the festival."

"Let's discuss it first thing in the morning after I've read the information you gave me. Right now I'd like to see Bob's work area."

"Back there." Helen gestured with her head to the hallway. "I'll show you."

The back door swung open, and Tommy burst into the room. "Mom, can we work at the big table? We don't have enough room at home for the project we're working on."

The young girl following Tommy towered over him; her straight-as-an-arrow ebony hair fell below her waist. Fred pushed his tubby body behind them through the doorway.

"Yes, you can work in here." Helen began to clear the table, then stopped and looked at me. "That is, if it's okay with Ms. Jackson."

"Of course, and please call me Kelly."

The girl took a paper from her purse. "Mrs. Rogers, check out my report card. My father's so proud. I had a D- in pre-algebra, and now it's a C+." She handed Tommy's mom the card.

Helen scanned the grades. "That's great."

"And it's all because of you, Tommy." The girl gave him a quick hug. His face went crimson, and his smile threatened to split his face. It was the first time I'd seen him so happy.

Fred's tail beat a drum solo on a table leg.

"I'm so lucky to have a really smart friend," the girl said.

"Al... Al... Allie, this is Miss Kelly." Tommy stuttered his way through introductions. "She works for the resort." He continued more calmly, "Miss Kelly, this is Allie, Daniel's daughter."

We shook hands. "Nice to meet you. Congratulations on your grade."

"It's awesome. He's in fifth-grade, and I'm in seventh, and he knows about everything I'm learning." She beamed at Tommy.

He ducked his head and fished a big book out of Allie's backpack. "We should get started."

Fred pawed Allie's knee.

"We'll play later, Fred. Promise." She rubbed his ears.

Helen straightened her tall, lean frame and signaled me to follow. A couple of short turns down a hallway, and Helen opened the door to Bob's office. She turned on the light and gasped.

Chapter 7

"I don't understand," Helen half-whispered. She gazed around the room that had been completely upturned. "Bob was meticulous when it came to keeping things organized. You'd think the head of the IRS worked here. Everything had a particular place on his desk, right down to his favorite pen. You saw more desktop than paper."

"It certainly doesn't look like that now." I scanned the room, taking in the mess.

"It wasn't like this earlier." Helen grabbed some papers and began to straighten them. "This is . . . awful."

"Wait!" My voice sliced through the air.

Helen stopped and stared at me.

"Sorry. I didn't mean to startle you, but I don't think we should touch anything." I paused. "The senior citizens' group, the Silver Sentinels, believe Bob was murdered."

"Murdered? Bob?" Helen dropped into a nearby chair. "Why would they ever think that?"

I recounted their reasons. "Now that someone has messed with the office, I think there's more cause to believe them."

Helen covered her face with her hands.

I walked over to her and placed my hand on her shoulder. "I know it's difficult to think someone might have killed Bob."

Helen's voice cracked. "Murder? Is it possible? And why?" She looked at me and shook her head. "Such a wonderful man."

I fished in my pocket and pulled out the deputy sheriff's card. "I'll call Deputy Sheriff Stanton and tell him what we've found."

Helen jerked upright and stood. "I'd better go check on the guests." She smoothed her tan slacks and left.

I took my cell phone out and punched in the number on the card. Two short rings, and he answered.

"Deputy Sheriff Stanton."

"Hi, Deputy Stanton, it's Kelly Jackson. We met this afternoon with the Silver Sentinels."

"Right."

"Helen and I just entered Bob's office. It looks like it's been searched. Helen said when she last saw it, everything was neat and organized. Now folders and papers are scattered around and some drawers are open."

"Were folders opened and dumped on the floor?"

I looked around. "No."

"Were files taken out of the cabinet and tossed around?"

"No."

"I assume there is a safe. Is it open?"

The manager's safe rested on a shelf to the left of the desk. I grabbed a tissue in case there were fingerprints and tried the handle. "It's locked."

"Is it messy like some college student's room?"

Definitely looked like mine in grad school. "Could be considered untidy like a student's."

"One of the staff was probably trying to find something."

"I thought you might want to investigate because of the Sentinels' belief he might have been murdered. Someone could've been searching for something."

"Ma'am, I have no suspicions Bob was murdered. He had an accident. I won't be sending anyone out. If you get anything else, please call."

"Wait!"

"Yes?"

"Bob had a BlackBerry that belongs to the company. I'd like to have that."

"I have an appointment with the coroner tomorrow. I'll check on it then."

"Thank you, Deputy Sheriff."

"You're welcome."

Helen entered the room with quiet, soft steps and stood at the door. "Is there anything you need?"

I hadn't thought she could appear any more haggard, but I was wrong. "I'd appreciate it if you'd bring a pair of latex gloves from the kitchen." It wouldn't hurt to preserve as much evidence as possible until I knew more.

"All right." She turned to go.

"Helen, Deputy Stanton feels an employee did this because they were trying to find something. Do you have any idea who that might be?"

Helen stopped. "No one said anything to me."

"Okay." I surveyed the mess. Where should I begin? "I need dinner, but I want to start putting these papers in order. Are there any fast, health-conscious restaurants nearby?"

"I can show you menus, and you can call ahead with an order." Helen hesitated a moment. "I'm going to make dinner for Tommy and me. Broiled chicken, rice, and steamed broccoli. Nothing fancy. I'd be happy to make some for you if you don't feel like going out."

I gave myself limited choices of what to eat. No red meat. Very little acceptable fish. Light in calories. Dinner out wasn't easy. And with Mom's cooking during my visit to the ranch making my jeans tighter than usual, it was more important than ever. I hadn't brought multiple sizes of clothing with me.

I jumped at the invitation. "Sounds great. It's sweet of you to offer."

Helen smiled and left.

I took out my phone and snapped photos of the disarray.

Helen returned with the gloves and placed them on the desk.

"Thanks."

"You're welcome. I'm going to get dinner started." She left, closing the door behind her.

I put on the gloves and sat in the chair. Was it a careless staff member or the murderer intent on finding something? Had the person found what they were after?

I shook the thoughts from my head and began to sort. The papers I needed to review went in one pile. The others remained as much where they were as I could manage. It wouldn't hurt to keep things as they were for the next day or so until we found out more about what happened.

I rolled the chair over to the safe. The resorts all had the same type. Some were just bigger than others. I spun the dial, ticking off the combination headquarters had provided, and opened the safe.

Taking the gloves off, I pulled out cash to count later, a stack of folders on the bottom shelf, and a large envelope. Most of the files were confidential documents on employees and contracts. I opened the envelope. It was labeled JOEY AND JERRY.

Pulling out the contents, I found pages of cryptic notes. *GAH-GHIL-KEID 4LS* was at the top of one and made no sense to me. Why would an inn manager leave notes in the safe that no one could understand? Was he afraid of what someone might find? What was it he was hiding?

I leaned back. Call the deputy sheriff? No. I could hear him now.

"You want me to examine indecipherable notes from an envelope labeled 'Joey and Jerry?' Why? Because a bunch of senior citizens think Bob might have been murdered and this might be a clue? No, Ms. Jackson, it's not going to happen."

Five pages into the documents was a handwritten note signed by Bob Phillips. *In case of my death, these documents are to be given to a representative of the Silver Sentinels.* A list of their names and phone numbers was attached. The Professor had "president" next to his name.

I think it's time to call my boss, Michael Corrigan.

I picked up the phone and dialed. I smiled when I heard Corrigan's hearty greeting.

"Hey, Kelly, how's it going? How was the flight into Mendocino County?"

"The ride was a roller-coaster experience. Not my favorite, as you know." I brought him up to speed on what had been happening.

"I agree with the police about Bob's death. Keep me posted if anything new comes to light."

"Will do. I found an envelope in the safe that doesn't appear to be related to Resorts International. I think it could be some investigation Bob was doing on his own. There's a note directing it to be turned over to the Silver Sentinels in the case of his death. May I do that?"

"Sure." He chuckled. "They sound like a crusty old group. I look forward to meeting them." His voice took on a different tone. "More power to them if there's any chance Bob's death wasn't accidental."

"Are you still planning to come on Saturday?"

"Yes. I'll arrive the morning of the chocolate and wine festival. Bob's memorial service is the next day. I'll stay at the company retreat. I'll see you Saturday."

The seven-acre company property was about ten miles inland. A perk for employees' families wanting a quiet getaway; a contemplative place for company representatives to meet.

"Call if you need anything," I said.

We said our good-byes and hung up. I enjoyed talking with my larger-than-life boss.

I pulled out the names and numbers Bob had left and dialed Herbert Winthrop.

"Professor, I have something for your group."

"So fast? My dear, you have a knack for finding things out."

"No, nothing like that. I opened the safe and found an envelope. There was a directive to hand it over to your group. I inspected the contents. Bob used a code or abbreviations for something he was researching. I talked to my boss. It doesn't appear to have anything to do with the business or Bob's family, and my boss was fine with turning it over to you."

"It would be our true pleasure to work on this. I can be there in about fifteen minutes."

"It's labeled 'Jerry and Joey.' Do you have any idea who they are?"

"Those are Bob's grandchildren."

"I wonder why he put their names on an envelope of encrypted notes?"

"I have no idea. The Sentinels will work on figuring that out. Is the conference room available?"

I examined a schedule mounted on the wall. "Yes."

"Very good, then. The group will assemble."

"I'll see you soon." I hung up.

Good. I could get on with my work. The Silver Sentinels had a project to sink their teeth into. If it led to a possible motive for killing Bob, maybe they had the information they needed for the police.

Helen returned carrying a tray with a covered plate, a glass of ice, and a tall bottle of Pellegrino, and placed it on a file cabinet.

"I can't tell you how much I appreciate this," I said.

Helen's face flushed. "I'm happy to help. Would you like anything else?"

"No thank you."

Helen twisted the dish towel tucked into her apron strings. "Thanks for the time you took with Tommy. He said he likes you. That means a lot, coming from him."

"I like him, too."

"If there's anything you need, just call. I'm on the automatic dialer. I have wine and cheese available for our guests until seven. People can call with questions until nine, and I keep the fire going until ten." She stopped and tugged at the towel. "I've been the person responsible for emergencies for the last two nights. Luckily, there haven't been any."

"Helen, emergencies are now my problem."

Helen's shoulders visibly relaxed. I pulled the file from the plastic container on the wall marked EMERGENCIES—a company requirement for all managers' offices.

I reviewed the plans. "I can handle this. Bob was a very organized individual."

"Yes, he was."

Heaviness returned to her voice. "I hope you enjoy your dinner."

"Thanks again for your hospitality. I'll see you in the morning."

Helen left, and I picked up the tray and placed it on the desk. There was a light knock on the door, and I opened it.

"Ahh, Ms. Jackson, so delightful to see you again." The Professor entered the room holding his gray wool cap in his hand. "The group is gathering. An impromptu potluck is creating itself. For better or for worse, Rudy is bringing his borscht. It all depends on your relationship with beets, you know. Love or hate."

I handed him the envelope of papers. "Bob used a note system that looks like a challenge to crack. Maybe the group can figure it out. If so, it might give you something to take to the deputy sheriff."

The Professor tucked the envelope under the arm of his brown tweed jacket. "We appreciate the fact that you take us seriously and are willing to help."

"I watched my grandfather deal with becoming 'invisible.' Your group is a wonderful role model." I sighed. "We have a young boy who blames himself for Bob's death. Not logical, but that's what he believes. If Bob was murdered, Tommy can let go of that guilt. And"—I looked at the slight, gray-haired gentleman—"we can catch a killer."

Chapter 8

After the Professor left, I began putting Bob's files back into the safe. I kept the employee folders and a few of the thicker vendor ones out to review in my room. As I closed the safe, I frowned, leaned forward, and examined its door. The small plate covering the keyhole was gone, and there were slight scratch marks. I searched for the missing piece and found it on the floor under the desk. I sat down in the chair, putting the piece next to the safe.

Should I call the deputy sheriff? I shook my head. *Nope. The safe wasn't open; there's nothing obvious missing. I will ask Helen when this room was last vacuumed. It might give us an idea of when the piece landed on the floor.*

I put the folders from the safe in my backpack, slung it over my shoulder, and picked up the dinner tray. As I passed the conference room, I noticed the door was open and the light on. Peeking in, I saw silver heads bent over the papers I'd given the Professor. The group's hastily assembled meal consisted of earthenware mugs filled with ruby red liquid, thick salami and cheese sandwiches piled on a plate, and a tray of lemon bars next to Mary Rutledge. The earthy smell of beets pervaded the room.

Rudy spied me at the door. "You are a true princess. Thank you so much for the treasure you've given us."

"Yah. We don't know yet," Ivan said, "but we solve it soon."

"Ms. Jackson, we've made progress!" The Professor held up a sheet of paper.

"Professor, please call me Kelly"—I smiled—"or I'll be using 'Mr. Herbert Winthrop.'"

"Quite. Kelly it is." His eyes twinkled. He nodded and pointed to some numbers. "We suspect these are dates, but that's as far as we've gotten. We'll let you know as soon as we learn anything more."

I put my things on the table and pulled out business cards from one of the backpack's zippered pockets. "This has my cell phone number on it." I handed one to each member. "Call if you find something."

"Would you like some of my famous borscht?" Rudy reached for a mug.

"I'll pass, but thanks for asking. Helen fixed me dinner." Besides, beets weren't one of my favorite foods. I picked up my things. "I need to do some paperwork."

"Honey, take some dessert with you," Mary's soft voice urged. "A gust of wind would blow you away."

"No thanks, but I appreciate the offer. They look great." I headed for the door. "Good luck with your deciphering."

A symphony of good nights followed me out of the room.

I flipped on my room lights and went into the kitchenette, putting the tray and my bag on the counter. A handwritten note next to the two coffee canisters proclaimed them to be MOUNTAIN JIM'S, THE BEST IN THE WEST, and gave directions. I poured decaf beans into the luxury coffeemaker. As the aroma of freshly ground coffee brewing filled the small living quarters, I uncovered the plate. An herb-covered chicken breast and thigh nestled between brown rice with sautéed mushrooms and vivid green broccoli dusted with Parmesan. Perfect. I carried the tray and paperwork to the sitting room and put them on the table. I opened the Pellegrino and poured the fizzling water into the glass of ice.

A swirling gray curtain of fog pushed against the panes of glass. I shivered, went to the gas fireplace, and switched it on. The warm glow pushed the chill away. I stifled a yawn, looking at my watch.

They went to bed early on the ranch, and their time zone was a couple of hours later. I thought I'd better call to see how Sis was doing. The babies were due two days ago.

I dialed the number, and my mother answered.

"Hi, Mom."

"Kelly, I'm so glad you called. I was beginning to worry."

I felt a rush of guilt. "I'm sorry. I've been trying to get up to speed here."

"You know me. Always the worrier." She paused. "It's hard to stop being a mother."

"I wouldn't want you to ever stop."

"And I promise I won't say any more about your new job."

Back to this. Mom couldn't understand why I left the family ranch to take the position with Resorts International. My need to prove myself. I visualized her straightening her back and doing her stiff-upper-lip routine.

"Just remember, there's always a job here for you," she added.

"I know, Mom."

"It's not charity, either. You're good at what you do."

"Thanks, Mom." Time to change the subject. "Any news on when the twins will make their grand entrance into this world?"

"No, but we're staying in town starting tomorrow until they're born."

"Good idea. How's Liz holding up?"

"Chipper as always." Mom laughed. "Her crazy Italian husband, on the other hand, is a basket case."

Dark-eyed, curly-haired Tony. He worshiped the ground my sister walked on.

I reached for my water. "I'm glad to hear she's okay."

"We'll call as soon as there's any news."

"Thanks, Mom. Love you."

"Love you, too."

"Tell Dad and everyone hi for me."

"Will do."

I snapped my phone shut.

The coffeemaker beeped. I found a mug and filled it with dark, aromatic liquid. As I took a sip, I decided the coffee deserved the title Best in the West.

Returning to the main room, I settled in to learn more about Redwood Cove Bed-and-Breakfast. I spread the paperwork out in front of me and took a bite of chicken. Tender, with a hint of fresh rosemary. I flipped through the folder labeled A TASTE OF CHOCOLATE AND WINE FESTIVAL as I ate. Resorts International donated the use of the inn's grounds. The Redwood Cove Artists organized the event. Plans for tables and tents, with rows neatly drawn and everything labeled, were provided, along with a use agreement. Lists of vendors, musical groups, and items for the silent auction were clipped to a note saying, "For your information" and signed by Ralph Peterson, Event Coordinator. The festival appeared to be good to go.

I finished the last piece of broccoli, grabbed my coffee and the remaining files, and went to the window seat. In spite of the warm room, I was chilled to the bone as damp wisps swirled by the window. A soft light green wool blanket was folded on the end of the seat. I settled into a corner of the cushions and pulled it up around me. Holding the hot mug between my hands, I thought about Bob's death.

The Sentinels seemed certain he was murdered, but there wasn't one shred of concrete evidence. The deputy sheriff figured an employee had disturbed the papers, looking for something. I reached for the staff folder and flipped through it. Employees were minimal— Daniel, Helen, and a small cleaning crew who'd been with the place for over twelve years. Bob and his wife rounded out the group.

The scratch marks took the situation to a deeper level. There had been no calls to the main office indicating a need for something in the safe. An attempted burglary? But who? I read the names on the list again. Daniel? Helen? I thought about Daniel's loving concern for Tommy and Helen's reaction upon opening the office door. I'd only just met them, but they seemed unlikely.

I didn't buy the deputy sheriff's take on what happened in the office. I felt even stronger about it with the discovery that someone had tampered with the safe. If Bob was murdered, then maybe he had something the person wanted—something that might be the proof they needed to find the killer.

I retrieved my room key, picked up the tray of dishes, and passed the now dark conference room. Dim lights illuminated the hallway. I entered the cavernous workroom and kitchen area and turned on the lights. I rinsed my plate and the utensils and put them in the dishwasher.

A loud *thud* from the parlor startled me.

I was about to investigate, then hesitated. There had been a lot of talk about murder today, and I believed the office had been searched. Had the person returned? No, if someone was after something Bob had, they'd already had a chance to search for it, so why return? I mentally pushed myself forward and my feet followed. The hallway's wooden floor creaked and groaned as I trod on its century-old boards.

I entered the living room. Several crystal lamps provided small pools of light. Their glow struggled to reach the room's far corners and failed. The high ceilings were cloaked in darkness.

Only a few glowing embers remained of the fire. One exploded, sounding like the crack of a rifle. I jumped, then chided myself for being so edgy. I walked farther into the room. A book lay on the floor next to a high-backed wing chair. An arm dangled over the chair's edge.

Chapter 9

I took in a deep breath as I walked around to the front of the chair. Andy Brown, the cheese connoisseur, sat slumped against the padded back.

Grabbing his arm, I shook it gently. No response. "Mr. Brown, wake up." I began to panic. A harder shake. "Wake up, Mr. Brown." Harder yet.

The man shouted.

I shrieked.

Andy's eyes flew open. "A samurai was bringing his sword down." He rubbed his face. "Good timing, Ms. Jackson. You saved me."

Relieved, I laughed. "I'm glad to hear it, Mr. Brown."

"Please call me Andy. I'm here a lot."

"And Kelly works for me."

He looked at the fireplace. "Mesmerizing. Before I dozed off, I was imagining what the Anderson family, the ones who built the house, would've been doing in the late eighteen hundreds. Reading the Bible? The missus knitting?" Andy checked his watch and rose. "Off to bed. Tomorrow's a busy day. The Happy Goats Cheese Company has new cheeses to sample." He grinned broadly. "Tough job, but someone's got to do it." He picked up his book and bid me good night.

His heavy footsteps echoed on the stairs, his breathing labored, and his hand slid on the rail as he headed for his room.

I checked the lock on the front door. A tree scraped its branches on the window—the scratching noises reminding me of the marks on the safe. Had it been attempted robbery? Or a murderer searching for something?

* * *

The next morning I sat at the workroom table crossing items off my to-do list. A couple of knocks sounded on the back door and Suzie gazed through the back door window.

She poked her head in. "Hi! Mind if I come in?" Her voice was as energetic as I remembered from the day before.

"Please do."

Suzie swung the door open. "FYI—most of the inn managers have an open-door policy. We drop in if we need something. Don't be surprised if you find an IOU in one of the cupboards. If that's a problem, I'll let the others know." Suzie smiled. "We take care of each other."

"Good to know." I returned the smile. "It's not often you see people in a competitive industry working as a community."

"It's a small town. We're all here together when the tourists are gone." Suzie sat at my table. "I'm sorry I had to leave yesterday before you got back. Issues at the hotel. I stopped by to see if you need anything."

"No problem. I'd like to find out what Bob was doing on Monday. It'll help me step into his shoes and understand this job better." I reached for my coffee. "Did you see him that day?"

"I did. Hey, why don't we talk about it over lunch, and I can introduce you to one of the locals' favorite spots to eat, Noah's Place."

"Sounds wonderful."

"We can circle through town, and I'll show you a couple of places your guests might like to visit."

"I'd love to." I didn't know how long I'd be managing the place, but it made sense to learn more about Redwood Cove.

"Will eleven work?"

"That's fine."

"See you then." Suzie waved her way out the door.

I read over my notes. Productive morning. I'd met the rest of the staff, made an appointment for three thirty with Phil Xanthis to sample new wines, and acquainted myself with the other suppliers Bob used. I'd called the hospital and found out Bob's wife had been taken off the intensive care list. Some good news for a change. I still had an hour before meeting Suzie. Time to write the report.

Helen came in with a load of napkin-covered baskets on a cart and put them on the counter, between the working area and the kitchen. "Good morning." She began taking dirty dishes out of the baskets.

"Let me help." Bob's wife had assisted with some of the chores, according to her job description. Her absence meant more work for Helen.

"Thanks, but I can manage." Helen started putting breakfast dishes into the dishwasher. "I'm sure you have a lot to do."

"I need to get a few things done, but there's time for that later." I admired the cheerful blue and white pattern on the dishes as I unloaded the containers. "Thanks for the breakfast you left outside the room. The almond croissant melted in my mouth."

"I'm glad you enjoyed it."

"Where did you get it?"

"I bake all the pastries from scratch."

"That takes a lot of skill. I know, having tried it once. *Once* being the operative word there."

Helen laughed. "I'd be happy to show you how."

"I might take you up on that." I emptied the last basket. "Right now it's report time."

We both looked around as a quick series of knocks on the door interrupted us.

Helen waved in a stout man in a chef's tunic. "Kelly, I'd like you to meet Jason Whitcomb."

"Hi, Jason. I'm Kelly Jackson, interim manager." I held out my hand, and Jason clasped it with a warm, moist grip and exercised my arm with energetic shakes.

"Glad to meet you." He put a box on the counter. "Helen, wait until you see what I brought."

"Jason and I love to bake and share recipes and ideas. He's been working on some creations for the chocolate and wine festival."

Jason appeared young, in spite of the streaks of gray hair at his temples. He had cheeks like apples—round and rosy. I figured many a mother was tempted to reach out and pinch them.

He grabbed a card out of his pocket and handed it to me. "I work in a restaurant in San Francisco on Mondays, Tuesdays, and Wednesdays. I bake for the Ralston Hotel Thursdays through Sundays. I'm building a catering business during the time I have between my shifts at the restaurant."

"Good to know you're available." I read the information on his card.

"Yeah. As soon as I'm making enough money, I want to move up here full-time." With a gleam in his eye, he turned to Helen, his hand hovering over the box's lid. "Are you ready?"

"Absolutely. You never cease to amaze, and I'm sure this time won't be any different," Helen replied.

With a dramatic flick of his hand, he pulled back the top, reached in, and pulled out a small tray.

"Ohh . . ." Helen breathed.

I took a step closer. Six cupcakes nestled together, but these weren't just any cupcakes. They were works of art. Each had a musical instrument on top. How did he make the strings for the violin? The keys for the piano? The stands for the drums?

"Those are incredible." I bent closer.

Jason rocked up and down on the balls of his feet. "Thank you. Thank you." He clapped his hands together and moved to get dishes from the counter. "There's more to come."

Jason placed a cupcake on each plate, and Helen handed him a knife. He cut one in half and pushed the sides apart. Chocolate oozed out from the center of the pastry.

"It's my version of a lava cake."

"Jason, you've outdone yourself." Helen handed me a fork.

"Thanks," he said. A Cheshire cat couldn't produce a bigger grin. "I decided on the instruments because I wanted to remind people the event is a fund-raiser for the Redwood Cove Music Festival."

"That's smart," Helen said.

"Taste. Taste," he urged me.

I took a bite and let the chocolate linger in my mouth. This man knew how to bake. "Excellent! Thanks for the treat."

Helen nodded in agreement, her mouth filled with cupcake.

"It was nice to meet you, Jason," I said. "I need to go get some work done. I look forward to sampling more on Saturday."

Back in my room, I started the computer, created a new Word document, and stared at the blank screen. The company wanted to know the circumstances of Bob's fall from my perspective and whether or not their pamphlets, which included things to avoid, should be changed.

I began typing. The spot where Bob fell would be considered safe by most coastal standards. In a few brief corporate-speak sentences, I described the scene and proposed that no changes be made in guest recommendations. I noted that an autopsy was being performed to see if an explanation, such as a heart attack, could account for the fall.

I printed a copy of the report, then pulled a folder from my brief-case labeled BOB PHILLIPS and opened it. It had his company employment information and a brief memo, stating he was found by a tourist at three thirty Monday afternoon. I placed the report in the file folder and put it in a file holder next to the computer. I attached what I had written to an e-mail and sent it off. The report wasn't the place to discuss my growing belief that Bob was murdered.

I put on my fleece and hat, making it to the kitchen just as Suzie knocked. I waved her in.

"Ready?"

"You bet." I followed her out.

Suzie walked fast, and I increased my pace to keep up.

"I'm going to take you to the Hudson House first. It was built in 1874 and has a museum and an interesting reference library."

"Great." I tightened my chin strap as a gust of wind threatened to dislodge my cowboy hat.

"I love your hat." Suzie glanced at it.

"Thanks. It was a gift from my family. My brothers got the horse-hair for the chin strap and the hatband. Grandpa wove the band, and Dad made the stampede string. My sister bought the hat, and Mom put it all together."

"Wow! That's neat. It's like they're all here with you."

"That was the idea." *That, and wishing me luck this job would be the one I could hang my hat on.*

Suzie stopped at a white-fenced yard. "I have a few distant cousins in Los Angeles. That's it." She pointed to a yellow ginger-bread-trimmed home. "This is Hudson House."

I stared at the building with its multiple roof peaks and inviting covered porch. "It appears really well-kept."

"Volunteers maintain the home and do an excellent job. They offer tours of the house and Redwood Cove. The Redwood Cove Visitors' Center is next. It's housed in a structure that was built in 1885."

"I appreciate the time you're taking to help me get acquainted with the area."

"Glad I can help." Suzie headed down the boardwalk.

"How long have you been in Redwood Cove?"

"About fifteen years." Suzie shoved her hands in her pockets. "I was living in Los Angeles. When I went through a nasty divorce, I decided on a complete change of scenery, and I wanted to get far, far away from my ex."

"I know all about difficult divorces."

We looked at each other. Unspoken communication about the depth of the pain and hurt passed between us.

"I ended up back at the family ranch."

"Where had you been living?"

"San Francisco. I went home and worked on the ranch. I ventured out a few times and tried several different jobs. I was a newspaper copy editor for a while, but I didn't like the hours. A stint as a travel agent didn't click. I got teaching credentials, thinking that would be a better fit. Nope. A class would end at six minutes after ten and another begin seven minutes later. You had twenty-eight minutes for lunch. Living a life by minutes wasn't for me. The kids were great though."

"How is it you came to be here?"

"Our ranch is a resort in the summer. People horseback-ride, hike, and fish. I helped out while I was growing up and again after the divorce. The family wanted me to stay and work there like my brothers and sister. I wanted something of my own. Dad knows Michael Corrigan, owner of Resorts International. He talked to him, and Corrigan gave me a temporary job in Colorado as an assistant. I helped with a difficult situation, and he promoted me to executive administrator. Here I am."

"Thanks for sharing." Suzie stopped in front of a modest white house, the United States flag whipping in the wind at the top of the pole in front of it. "This is the Redwood Cove Visitors' Center. It has information about the area as well as exhibits. They lead a variety of walks. The north side of town borders the cove, and most of the land around it is parkland."

I was glad we'd stopped. Between my talking and our fast pace, I needed a chance to catch my breath.

"There are more places to see, but it's time to head to Noah's Place. I need to get back to work soon." Suzie pointed across the street. "That's the Ralston Hotel, where I'm general manager. We can cut through over there, and you can see more of the town."

The building she indicated was a lovely Victorian with wood shingle siding in a scalloped pattern skirting the bottom of the building. The upper part of the hotel displayed traditional vertical boards. The chosen color was cream with white trim. The lush vegetation spoke to the optimal coastal weather conditions for plants.

Locals, many with long hair and ragged jeans, were easily distinguished from visitors. Whenever one saw Suzie, there was a wave or a nod. She led me to a light yellow building with black trim, then opened the screen door and held it for me.

We found a place in the back with menus between salt and pepper shakers. Staff bustled among the tables. The rich smell of baking pizza and the happy chatter of locals and tourists enveloped me. A young boy eating, as well as wearing, his ice cream leaned against his mother's leg. I surveyed the list and determined it was raspberry chocolate fudge by the colors on his T-shirt.

"They have lots of pizza choices, salads, and vegetarian options. Most of the ingredients are organic." Suzie scanned the menu. "The ice cream is locally made. They have twenty flavors daily and rotate the offerings." She put the menu down.

"Hey, Suz, how's it going?" A young man with a sunny smile, tie-dyed shirt, and well-worn jeans came to the table. His almost-shoulder-length dark brown hair was tucked behind his ears.

"Noah, I'd like you to meet Kelly Jackson. She's managing the Redwood Cove Bed-and-Breakfast for a while."

"Nice to meet you." A cloud passed over his face. "Any news on Ruth?"

"She's out of intensive care," I said.

"Glad to hear it." Noah pursed his lips and took out a pad and pen from his back pocket. "What can I get you ladies?"

"I'll have two slices of the Apprentice," Suzie said, "and a pot of tea."

I read the menu. The Apprentice pizza listed roasted garlic sauce, mushrooms, tomatoes, chicken, and caramelized onions all topped with fresh basil.

"Any suggestions?" I scanned the choices.

He cocked his head at me. "You might want to try the grilled portobello mushroom burger. Like nothing else on the planet."

The description of Noah's burger won me over. Organic mushroom caps marinated in balsamic vinegar and fresh rosemary, among other wonderful seasonings. Toppings included grilled red onions, avocado, spinach, tomatoes, and pepper jack cheese. A seasonal green salad came on the side. "Burger it is, and I'll have tea, as well."

"Got it." Noah went to a side bar and came back with a wide array of organic teas from New Way Tea Company.

"You wanted to know about my meeting with Bob." Suzie put the tea bag into the pot that had whizzed to our table in record time.

"Please." I placed my purple napkin in my lap and pulled my notebook from my fanny pack.

"Bob came over because he wanted to review the details for the chocolate and wine festival one more time. His thoroughness was legendary." Her smile was a quiet one, not the usual bright burst I'd become accustomed to. "We also help with breakfast baking when your inn is as full as it is now. We were discussing pastry choices. Bob was conscientious about having new offerings for the guests."

"I talked with the wine merchant, Phil. He said the same thing."

"Bob worked hard to build a loyal clientele."

"Do you know where Bob was before he met you or where he was going afterward?"

"No, we didn't talk about it."

"What time did he meet with you?"

"It was eleven. Speaking of the festival, I need to show you where some of the food is going to be stored and give you a couple of keys. Would tomorrow morning work?"

"It should. I don't know the routine at the inn yet to feel comfortable setting a time right now. I'll give you a call in the morning."

"Sounds good."

A waiter arrived and placed food on the table. Suzie's pizza had mounds of mushrooms; thinly sliced caramelized onions dripped over the sides of the slices. My burger was a riot of color accompanied by a vibrant green salad on the side.

Suzie was a local. She'd know about the Silver Sentinels. I wondered how she felt about them. "There's a group of senior citizens called the Silver Sentinels." I sipped my tea. "Do you know them?"

"Yes. I think they're a nice group of old folks looking for something to do."

I poured myself more tea. Should I say something about their belief that Bob was murdered? If rumors were going around, she'd probably heard them. Maybe others besides the Sentinels had the same thought. It was worth asking. "They believe Bob was murdered. What do you think? Have you heard anything?"

"Murdered?" Melted cheese dripped from her pizza onto the plate as she held it still. "No, I haven't heard anything like that. Who do they think did it?"

"They don't have any suspects. They feel Bob wouldn't have an accident like that."

"Accidents do happen, even to experienced people." She took a bite of pizza, then set the piece on her plate. "Like I said, a nice group of people looking for something to do."

I took a bite of my lunch. I relished the blend of flavors and textures produced by the salad, the grilled mushrooms, and the accompaniments. "When Helen and I checked Bob's office, there were a lot of papers scattered over his desk. Helen felt it was unusual."

"His office a mess? Never."

I nodded. "That was Helen's feeling. I talked to Deputy Sheriff Stanton about the office being searched. He thinks an employee was likely trying to find something."

"Maybe." Suzie finished her first slice. "I don't know who it would be, though. I was handling most of the business issues. Our suppliers were pretty much the same. I did the inn's orders when I did mine. Daniel knows a bit, but Helen is pretty clueless. I can't think of anything they or anyone else would be looking for."

I didn't realize how isolated I'd been feeling. Hearing Suzie mirror my doubts reassured me. An ally.

"What do you think?" Suzie asked.

"I think someone was searching for something. Did you see anyone go in Bob's office yesterday afternoon?"

Suzie thought for a moment. "Charlie Chan."

Chapter 10

Noah put the bill on the table. "How was it?"

"Wonderful!" I said. "A creative menu that delivers. What more could someone ask for?"

"I'm glad you enjoyed it." He cocked an eyebrow at Suzie. "Music here tonight. It'll be the Road Travelers playing. Good stuff."

Suzie laughed. "We'll see how things go at work."

We paid the bill, thanked Noah, and left.

"There's Charlie." Suzie pointed down the narrow alley at the back of the restaurant.

As we walked toward the young man unloading his truck, my cell phone rang.

"Hello."

"The deputy sheriff returned Bob's cell phone. Should I put it in the office desk?" Helen asked.

"That works for me. The center drawer of the desk will be fine. Thanks." I closed the phone. "The sheriff dropped off Bob's Black-Berry. That should help me track his movements."

Charlie glanced in our direction. "Hey, how're you doing?" The future dentist displayed his perfect teeth.

"Hi." I slipped the phone into my backpack. "Charlie, I have a question for you."

"Sure, shoot." He heaved one of the large bottles off the truck and placed it near the back door of Noah's Place.

"When you went in Bob's office yesterday, did you notice what his desk looked like?"

Charlie didn't look at me. "No." He grabbed another jug and turned to me. "Why?" The smile was gone.

I faltered. Why, indeed? If I was going to question people to try to figure out if they'd searched the desk, I needed to have a reason. I snatched the first thought that entered my mind. "We're trying to track down some paperwork." I paused. "You've been in the office before. I thought you might have noticed something."

"I haven't been with the company that long." He took off his gloves. "Sorry."

"Thanks anyway."

Suzie and I said good-bye and walked down a rutted gravel road toward the inn.

"I appreciate the information you've given me and the assistance you've given Helen and Daniel."

"Happy to do it."

The sound of a rattling car engine approaching us interrupted the conversation.

"Would you two like a lift?" Daniel pulled alongside us in a faded blue Volkswagen van.

"We're fine walking," I replied. "I'm getting a lesson in local history."

"Thanks for asking, Daniel." Suzie smiled.

"You're welcome." The vehicle sputtered down the road.

"He and Bob tinkered on that thing for hours together. Daniel's love. Bob's way to be with him." Suzie seemed to be ready to say more but stopped and shoved her hands into the pockets of her red jacket. Her blond ponytail swung with her long strides.

"Were they close?"

"Daniel was one of Bob's 'saves.' He was always the first to step forward when someone needed help." She shook her head. "Daniel's wife left him, clearing out their bank account, taking most everything except for the VW and . . . Allie. Bob loaned him the money to keep the house and hired him full-time when the opportunity presented itself."

I imagined the pain Daniel felt. Too easy to remember the aching heart. I wasn't ready to go down the relationship path again anytime soon. And Allie, how devastating for her.

"Here's where I split off," Suzie said.

"Thanks for taking me to Noah's Place."

"You're welcome." Suzie waved. "If you need anything, let me know."

We parted. The tall Victorian steeple of the B&B on the next block was framed by a sky dotted with small puffs of white and the blue-green ocean in the background. Had Charlie been lying? The happy persona he displayed had disappeared for an instant.

I glanced to my left. Tommy, Allie, and several boys were on the far side of the empty lot I was passing. Tommy's bike was on the ground, his legs spread apart, his fists clenched as he faced the boys. The ever-present Fred sat next to him. As I watched, Allie put her bike down and stood next to Tommy. She jabbed her finger at the boy in front and leaned down toward him. Allie was a commanding head taller than any of them. I decided to detour in their direction, following a dirt path through the weeds.

As I got closer, Tommy's flushed face became more pronounced and Allie's yelling became clearer. Allie took a step closer to the boy, towering over him. "You leave him alone, or you'll have me to deal with."

Fred's doleful eyes rolled in my direction, and he wagged his tail.

"And my dog's not a retard," Tommy shouted. His white-knuckled fists curled even tighter.

"What's going on, guys?" I asked with my schoolteacher voice.

"He was going to hit Fred with a stick." Tommy's face was blotched red and white.

"No, I wasn't," said a chunky boy in a gray T-shirt that sported a picture of a skull with flaming eyes. "I was only messin' with you." He tossed the branch he'd been holding.

"What's your name?"

He scowled at me from under heavy dark eyebrows.

"Micky Donovan," Allie spat out.

"I'm Kelly Jackson, Micky. Tommy works for my company. Fred's the inn's mascot." Okay. I was inventing a bit. "If I hear of you doing anything to either of them, I'll not only contact your parents, but I'll let the deputy sheriff know."

"C'mon, guys. Let's go." Micky shot me a mean look. The one in black leather with chains, greasy hair, and acne peeking through the strands moved away. The younger, plumper version of Micky followed.

"And, Micky," said Allie, "remember what I said. Tommy's my friend. You mess with him, you mess with me. And another thing, your trick with the e-mails to get me in trouble didn't work."

"I don't know what you're talking about." He sneered at her.

"I got called in to the principal's office because teachers had been getting nasty e-mails supposedly from me. You snuck up behind me when I was logging on this morning in computer class, and I bet you saw my password."

"Did not." His eyes shifted from side to side.

"The principal knows it's not me because you sent one of the e-mails when I was talking with my math teacher, Mrs. Owens. I told him what happened in the computer lab. He'll be calling you in for a talk." She placed both hands on her hips. "So there!"

"Like I said, I didn't do anything." His sullen voice lacked conviction. "Let's get out of here," he said to his friends.

The boys walked off, their steps stiff and awkward. Any attempt at being nonchalant failed.

"You kids okay?" I asked.

"Yes, Miss Kelly," Allie replied. "They're a group of bullies. Turn tail and run if anyone fights back."

"Allie." Tommy opened and closed his fists. "Did you mean what you said to Micky? That he's got you to deal with if he tries anything?" His face began to regain its natural color.

"You bet. We're buds." She grinned at him. "Though, on second thought, that depends on how much algebra we can get through before tomorrow."

Tommy picked up his bike, and Allie did the same.

"And I need help changing my e-mail password."

"You got it," Tommy said. "Thank you, Miss Kelly."

The two jumped on their bikes and raced toward the B&B.

The gut-wrenching anguish of growing up. Red hair had been my bane. Redheaded woodpecker. Carrot top. Tomato head. Tormentors and the tormented.

When I got back to the inn, Tommy and Allie's bikes were resting on the side of Helen and Tommy's cottage. I opened the back door of the B&B, and warm air scented with afternoon baking rushed out. Helen was rinsing grapes.

She looked over her shoulder. "How was lunch?"

"Good food and enjoyable company." I put my fanny pack on the table. "Suzie's a sweet person, and Noah's Place is a lot of fun."

"It's one of the few places where locals and tourists mix." Helen put the grapes in a colander. "No airs and affordable."

I sat down at the counter. "On my way back, I found several boys confronting Tommy and Allie." I explained what had taken place.

"Like sharks smelling blood." She turned the water up and vigorously washed another bunch of grapes. "Hint of someone a little different, and they're after him." Helen plunked them down next to the other ones.

She twisted the water off with such force I thought the knob might snap.

"He has a staunch friend in Allie."

"She's been a godsend." Helen covered the grapes with plastic wrap.

"I don't think those boys will bother Tommy again."

"Allie and Tommy have really helped each other." She put the fruit in the refrigerator. "She was failing in school and getting in fights." Helen reached into a cupboard and took down dessert plates. "You heard her yesterday. Completely turned around."

"She certainly was a bundle of happiness."

Helen pulled out silver forks and knives. "She's gaining so much confidence in herself. It's a pleasure to watch."

"I'm going to get the BlackBerry and see what I can find out."

The Oriental runner muted my steps as I went down the dim, windowless corridor. Would the phone reveal anything of interest? I stopped in front of the office, reached for the antique metal doorknob, and gave it a twist. I pushed the massive oak door open and walked toward the desk.

A violent blow was delivered between my shoulder blades, and I catapulted forward. I slammed into the floor, and a sharp pain erupted as my head grazed the side of the desk. The door closed. I felt like I was suffocating. I couldn't breathe. I willed my arms to move. Nothing.

Chapter 11

I desperately tried to take in air. My heart raced as my lungs cried out for oxygen. *Stop struggling. This feels like what happened when you fell off that crazy horse and had the wind knocked out of you.* I willed myself to be still. After a few seconds, which seemed like an eternity, I could take in a shallow breath. Others followed. I sent a signal to my arm to move. It finally began to inch upward. A glance around the room showed it to be empty.

Grabbing the edge of the oak desk, I pulled myself up, using all the energy I could muster, and gingerly touched my scalp. A lump had started to form. I examined my finger, and there was a spot of blood. Pulling back my shirtsleeves, I realized there'd be bruises, but the skin wasn't broken. I opened the desk drawer. No BlackBerry.

I closed the drawer and sat in the chair, resting my head in my hands. What could be so important on the phone that someone would steal it? What had Bob entered that made someone feel so threatened?

Fluffing my bangs over the scrape and buttoning my shirtsleeves hid the damage. I walked back to the kitchen, taking small steps, collecting my thoughts and myself. I knew from ranch incidents that the shove made it an assault, a felony. Someone really wanted that mobile device.

Helen stood at the work counter, arranging pieces of blue-veined cheese on a crystal platter.

"Helen, did anyone come through this room just now?"

"No." She placed a brick of golden-hued cheese on the cutting board, picked up a knife, and began slicing. "I've been here since you left, and there's been no one."

"Who was in the same room with you when you called me about the BlackBerry?"

Helen glanced up, a questioning look on her face. She thought a moment. "I was here in the work area. Phil and Andy were planning the chocolate and wine event. Jason brought some pastries to help with the full house we have this weekend. Daniel was helping a couple of the produce deliverymen." She shrugged her shoulders. "That's it." A frown creased her forehead. "Why?"

"The BlackBerry isn't in the drawer."

"That's impossible." She put her knife down and headed for the hallway. "I put it there myself."

"Wait. There's more."

Helen stopped and turned.

I wanted to keep the attack to myself, but I knew Deputy Sheriff Stanton would be asking questions. She'd find out sooner or later.

"Someone shoved me to the floor. I didn't see who it was. They were hiding behind the door when I opened it."

"Oh my gosh. Are you okay?" She hurried over to me.

"I have a few bruises. That's about it."

"Who could've done such a thing?" Helen's face drained of color.

"Is the front door left unlocked?"

"During the day, yes. We've never had a problem, and it's easier for the guests."

"I'm changing the policy. They'll need to take their keys with them from now on."

"What will we tell people?"

"I'm not sure. I'll think about it." I grabbed my bag. "I need to call the deputy sheriff and my boss, Michael Corrigan."

"Can I get something for you? Is there anything I can help you with?" Helen hovered.

"No, I'll be fine. Thanks."

I went back to my room and took some ice cubes out of the freezer, wrapped them in a towel, and gently held the pack against my head. I sank down on the window seat. Time to make my calls. *Maybe this will convince the sheriff something's wrong.* I put the ice down and dialed his number on the room phone.

"Deputy Sheriff Stanton."

"Deputy, Kelly Jackson here."

"Yes, Ms. Jackson, how can I help you?"

I explained what happened.

"Sorry, ma'am. There are a lot of people out of work in this area. It's a hand-to-mouth community in many ways. I expect someone saw an opportunity for a few extra bucks."

I felt the sigh from him more than heard it.

"Tourist areas suffer when the economy struggles. People see the beautiful hotels and fancy shops." The deputy paused. "There's a whole different layer wrapped in desperation. An ugly underbelly lies beneath some of those houses with gingerbread trim."

"Deputy Sheriff, the office appears to have been searched. It looks like an attempt to break into the safe took place, and Bob's BlackBerry has been stolen. The shove makes it a felony. Don't you feel this incident is one more thing to point in the direction that maybe the Silver Sentinels are correct and Bob's death is suspicious?"

This time the sigh was more audible. "No. Petty crime isn't uncommon in this area. I think you were in the wrong place at the wrong time, and whoever it was didn't want to get caught. The person saw a chance to shove and run."

Stonewalled. "Okay, Deputy Sheriff Stanton." I reined in the sarcasm and bit back the words struggling to come out. Alienating local law enforcement wasn't a good idea.

"Was anything else taken?"

Oops. I hadn't checked. "I don't know. I'll check."

"I'll come by and get more details from you and make a report. I can be there in about half an hour."

"I plan on being in the rest of the afternoon."

"And, Ms. Jackson, don't hold your breath about getting the BlackBerry back. It's probably headed for Saturday's flea market in Santa Rosita."

"Got it."

"See you in a bit." He ended the call.

No connection? Too many coincidences were just that. Too many to be happenstance. In addition, Bob had a group of friends who'd known him for years saying he was murdered. His death was looking less and less like an accident.

Now it was time for Corrigan. Having a robbery to deal with and a possible murder was not the plan for my first assignment. I picked the ice pack up, placed it on my forehead, and auto-dialed his number on my cell phone.

"Hi, Kelly, how's it going? I read your report. Well done."

"Thanks. I want to give you an update. Deputy Sheriff Stanton left Bob's BlackBerry here . . . and someone stole it."

"What happened?"

"Helen put it in the desk drawer. When I went to get it, it was gone."

"What does Bill think?"

Oh great, he knows the deputy. "He thinks it was someone grabbing what they could to pick up a few bucks."

"He's probably right. Bill's got a good finger on the pulse of the community."

I'll definitely need more facts to present to Michael before I suggest there's a possible connection between the ransacked office, the stolen BlackBerry, and Bob's death.

"This inn has an open-door policy. I made the decision to change that. Guests will need to carry their keys." I held my breath. It was the first administrative decision I'd made.

"Good idea."

I let my breath out. Approval.

"There's more." I dreaded telling him about the attack. Michael had been very protective in the past. I didn't want to be taken off the job. "I surprised the robber. When I went into the office, I was shoved from behind."

"What! Are you okay?"

"I'm fine. I have a few bruises, but I used to get plenty of those working on the ranch."

"There's been a theft, and you've been assaulted. I'm sending another manager out to help. Scott finished the job he's been on and can be there by tomorrow."

Scott. A walking cliché—tall, dark, and handsome, looking like he walked off the cover of a romance novel. We'd worked together briefly in Colorado.

"No, not . . . not Scott," I stammered. Clenching the phone, I made myself enunciate each word clearly. "Please don't send anyone. It wasn't about me. Deputy Sheriff Stanton feels the person just wanted to get away and saw an opportunity."

"Why don't you want me to send someone?"

"If Scott was here instead of me, would you send a second person?"

Silence.

"I can handle this."

The silence lengthened.

"I understand," Michael finally said. "Okay."

"Nothing else will happen. Everything will be fine from here on out." At least, I hoped that was the case.

Chapter 12

I leaned back. Two wins—my first administrative decision and Corrigan not sending Scott. Michael's trust felt good. I was shaping a place for myself in the organization.

What didn't feel good was the sudden stabbing pain in my forehead. I reached for my bag and took out some aspirin. I shook two pills out of the bottle, went to the kitchen, and filled a glass with water. After taking the medicine, I went to lie on the bed.

Who shoved me? Who knew about the BlackBerry? Helen said Daniel, Andy, Jason, and Phil, as well as a couple of workers from the produce store, were present when she phoned me. Charlie Chan had been close enough to hear my conversation with Suzie. Helen and Suzie knew, of course. I doubted the deputy sheriff would mention it to anyone but staff. And two break-ins at the office. Someone wanted something. If it wasn't the BlackBerry, then whatever it was, I planned on finding it first.

My cell phone rang, and I checked who was calling. Scott! Had Corrigan called him? It rang again. Did this mean he was coming here after all?

"Hello." My stomach churned.

"Hi, Kelly."

It was an upbeat voice I remembered well.

"Congratulations on your new position."

"Thanks, Scott," I said warily, wondering what was next.

"I wanted to let you know I'm familiar with that inn. I've been there numerous times. If you have any questions, please give me a call. I'm happy to help."

Upbeat *and* helpful. This man must have a flaw, though I hadn't found it when we worked together before.

"Thanks for the offer. Everything at the inn is running smoothly so far." *It isn't a lie*. The incidents in the office weren't connected with managing the day-to-day business of the B&B.

"I'm glad you're part of our administrative team. We have quarterly meetings. I look forward to seeing you at them."

"I look forward to seeing you, too." Did I? The turmoil I felt was a different one from when I answered the phone. I glanced at the clock. "I've gotta run. I have an appointment in a few minutes." I didn't add that it was with a deputy sheriff.

"Keep in touch. 'Bye."

"I will." *I won't*. "Good-bye."

I'm not ready for a relationship. I'm not ready for a relationship. I muttered the phrase over and over as I went to the door.

The good news was that Corrigan had kept his word.

The phone's ringing startled me awake. I lifted the receiver.

"Hello?"

"Kelly, how are you feeling?" Helen asked.

"I'm fine. Just a little sore."

"Phil's here to meet about the wine. Should I tell him you'll reschedule?"

I paused for a moment. After-adrenaline-rush exhaustion consumed me after meeting with the deputy sheriff, and I'd crawled in bed. The short nap helped. My watch said three thirty. Still a lot of day to go.

"I'll see him. Please tell him I'll be there in a few minutes."

"Okay."

I peered at my reflection in the bathroom mirror. The bruises were covered by my sleeves. The lump didn't show under my bangs, and a few strokes of the brush put my hair back in place. I straightened my blouse and left to meet the wine merchant.

As I walked to the kitchen, I reflected on my meeting with Deputy Sheriff Stanton. He hadn't budged on his thoughts. He was like a mule that had decided it was done working for the day. It hadn't helped that Helen noticed some loose change had been swiped, as well.

Entering the work area, a man in loose black slacks, a white shirt open at the collar, and an unbuttoned vest patterned with intertwining green and gold vines was setting out a row of wineglasses. He bent over to arrange a napkin. His head was covered with tightly coiled springs of short, gray hair. Several uncorked bottles were on the table. He whistled a song, slow at first, then suddenly speeding up. He executed a swirling dance step and held a glass high.

He spun around and saw me. "Ah, welcome. I'm Philopoimen Xanthis. You must be Ms. Jackson."

"Please call me Kelly. It's a pleasure to meet you." We shook hands.

"Call me Phil for both our sakes. My mother got carried away when she went searching for a traditional Greek name."

I eyed the table setting. "How many are we expecting for this tasting?"

Phil appeared puzzled. "I only planned on the two of us. Have others been invited?"

"I asked because of the number of glasses."

"We're doing a flight of merlots. That's three glasses for each of us."

"What is a flight of merlots?"

"We'll have small tastes of three wines from the same family, produced in different years."

"It's only three thirty in the afternoon."

"Yes?" Phil looked at me in confusion.

"Isn't it early to be tasting wine?"

"Early?" He appeared startled at the concept. "This is California wine country. And in the old country we . . ." He shook his head. "Early, no."

I leaned down and examined the wine label. It displayed a slender, elegant-looking greyhound sitting upright with a flowing red scarf encircling its throat. A wing was folded along its side, reminding me of the winged horse, Pegasus. At the upper right corner of the label was a tiny gold emblem of a flying dog.

"Please sit." He gestured toward a chair at the table.

He arranged three glasses in front of me, setting each down with careful precision.

"These wines are from a boutique estate winery, The Flying Dog, not far from here."

"Phil, I know very little about wine. What kind of winery is that?"

"The estate part refers to the fact they do everything on site, including bottling and labeling. Boutique means they don't produce a lot. This winery does fifteen hundred to two thousand cases a year. All organic."

"Interesting."

"This is a 2001 merlot. You'll notice rich flavors of red cherries and dark plums." He poured a little into two glasses and handed me one. Picking his up, he swirled the glass and took a sniff.

I followed his lead.

Phil sipped and nodded his head. "No surprise it's a gold medal winner."

It was a pleasant wine, but the subtle differences in flavors were lost on my untrained palette.

"Now we cleanse our taste buds with bread dipped in olive oil." He poured gold liquid into two small bowls and took a piece of cubed bread from a plate in the middle of the table. "Handpicked organic olives are used for this oil. The winery makes this as well." He pressed the bread into the oil and placed it in his mouth, seemed to roll the chunk around, and swallowed. I did the same.

He described and poured the second wine.

"Do you and Andy plan cheese and wine pairings for the inn?"

"Yes. We've worked together for years." He swirled, sniffed, and sipped. "A number of inns and resorts follow our recommendations."

I took a drink, then dutifully cleansed my taste buds. How could I find out where Phil was earlier this afternoon when the BlackBerry was taken?

"You have an interesting job. What's a typical day for you?" I reached for another piece of bread. "Like, what did you do today, for example?"

"Handled e-mails and phone calls first thing in the morning. I deal with vendors across the United States and Europe. I met with Andy about the festival. We were going to have lunch together, but one of his appointments got changed to one, and we had to cancel. Left some sample wines at several places, then back here to meet you." He poured the third wine.

Andy and business stops. That didn't help much. Where was he at one thirty? Maybe I could find out.

"Do you like all the driving you have to do?"

"Love it. No sitting behind a desk. I have an office in Petaluma but spend very little time there. Travel around one of the most beautiful areas in the world, talk wine, taste wine." He laughed. "What more could you ask for?"

"Sounds great. Where did you travel to this afternoon?"

It was the best I could come up with. I waited for him to ask me why I wanted to know. My sleuthing skills needed a lot of work.

"Only to Fort Paul."

That didn't get me the specifics I wanted. Time to leave it alone and rethink my approach before he got suspicious. Maybe I could find out from Andy.

"What do you think?" Phil rubbed his hands together after the last pour. "Do you have a favorite?"

"I can taste differences, but I'm not a connoisseur, and I don't know enough about the clientele here to know what they expect." I took a last sip and put my glass down. "How long had you worked with Bob?"

"About two years."

"You have a much better idea about what he would choose. You pick."

"He wasn't about playing it safe by going with the mildest wine. Bob wanted people to notice there was something special in what they tasted." He surveyed the bottles. "These are all within the price range he requested." He paused. "I think he would've gone with the second one. Distinct taste, but not as much oak as the last one."

"Sounds fine to me."

"Done. I'll order three cases." He began to clean up, whistling once again.

I recognized the melody. "'Never on Sunday,'" I blurted. Folk dancing had been a favorite of mine in high school.

Phil nodded and executed a few Greek line-dance steps.

"Hi, everyone." Daniel came in, carrying a couple of grocery bags, which he placed on the counter. He walked over to me, concern in his eyes. "How are you feeling? Helen told me you were attacked."

"I'm fine. Only a few bruises."

"Attacked?" Phil's eyebrows almost caught up with his receding hairline. "What happened?"

"Shoved is more accurate." I recounted the story. It was probably the highlight of afternoon community gossip by now.

"Heavens. We could certainly have postponed our tasting." Phil tut-tutted as he put the wine bottles in a box.

"I'm glad we met. I learned a lot. Thank you."

"You're welcome." Phil carried glasses to the sink. "Any time."

Daniel began unpacking the bags. "Helen asked if I saw anyone. I didn't. I was outside most of the time."

"I'm going back to my room to read some of the files." I left.

My cell phone rang as I reached my door.

"We solved it. We cracked the code!" an excited, rapid voice exclaimed.

Chapter 13

I barely recognized the Professor's voice.

"Navajo Code Talkers," he spluttered.

"Who?"

"Bob was a WWII buff." He enunciated clearly this time. Some of the Professor's calm demeanor was returning. "The Navajos used their unwritten language to transmit information. Many believe they hastened the end to the war, and the marines probably wouldn't have taken Iwo Jima without them."

"Bob was using the Navajo code in his notes?"

"Correct."

"But if it's unwritten . . ."

"The military made a dictionary. It was declassified in '68."

"What did you learn?"

"Bob discovered an abalone poaching gang. It's a huge operation. Can we use the conference room to meet with a Fish and Game warden?"

"I'll check availability and get back to you." My excitement was building. Navajo code? Abalone poaching? It sounded like a scene from a movie. I went to the computer. A couple of clicks later I determined the room was available. I typed in *Silver Sentinels* and blocked the space.

I grabbed my phone and punched in his number. "Professor, the room's yours."

"I'll let Fran Cartwright with Fish and Game know. Hopefully, she can meet with us. We'll be there in an hour or less."

"Professor, my congratulations to the Sentinels for breaking the code."

"Thanks. Maybe this is connected to Bob's murder."

There was that word again, *murder*. But now, after all that had happened, I was ready to believe it. Still, what was the motive? Did abalone poaching net enough money to kill for? And who? Was it one of the poachers or someone else? I didn't think it was random. Maybe in a big city. Small town, unlikely.

I went to the work area and started to pull water glasses from the top shelf of the cupboard. My bruised muscles protested as I struggled to reach them.

Daniel came in with a log carrier full of wood. "Hi." He put the canvas sack down. "Is there something I can help you with?" The fresh air of the outdoors clung to him.

"Thanks for the offer. I need four more glasses."

"No problem."

"The Silver Sentinels are coming over. I want to put out water and some snacks." I opened the refrigerator and examined the possibilities. Gouda, a dark cheddar, and some local goat cheese were on the top shelf. I reached in and pulled out the cheddar.

"What are they up to this time?" Daniel asked.

I hesitated. The group had no proof, and I didn't want to stir people up. However, I'd already told Helen and Suzie about the Sentinels' suspicions. It would get to Daniel eventually, if it hadn't already. "They think Bob was murdered and are trying to figure out why." No reason to mention the envelope of papers.

Daniel frowned, took down a couple of glasses, and put them on a nearby tray. "Remember when we were at the accident site and you asked if there was anything else?"

"Yes." I chose English water crackers and organic wheat thins from the supply of boxes on the work counter and then slid a platter out of the rack next to the stove.

"The Sentinels had talked to me. I didn't feel comfortable saying anything about their thoughts at the time. It seemed like such a stretch." He took down two more glasses and paused. "If a man could exist with no enemies, it was Bob."

"So you don't think he was murdered?"

Daniel came over and stood next to me. I never think of myself as short until someone tall stands beside me, and Daniel was tall.

"I just can't imagine it. But . . . strange things happen in life." He looked at me. "They're a good group and bright. In the Indian culture, age is wisdom. Unfortunately, less so in the White world. I'd listen to them."

I studied the high cheekbones and straight black hair. "Do you have a Native American background?"

"I'm part Lacoda. They originally populated this area. Now there are about two hundred left. They live on the Lacoda Indian Reservation near here."

"Do you have relatives there?"

He laughed quietly. "No. Gone many years ago." Daniel placed napkins next to the glasses. "I want Allie to understand our heritage. She's learning the language from one of the elders and participating in some of the ceremonies."

"That's wonderful." I arranged cheese slices on the dish and put the remainder of the brick of cheddar next to them. I washed my hands and wiped them on a dish towel. "What a great experience for her."

"She's enjoying it. That's what counts."

"Thanks for your help and for the information about the Sentinels."

He grinned. "And thanks for *your* help."

"What do you mean?"

"I heard about the altercation with Allie, Tommy, and the young thugs, as Allie refers to them." He shook his head. "Allie has a past to overcome."

"What kind of past?"

"There was a time not long ago when she got into lots of fights." Daniel turned away and filled a pitcher with water. "The school district has her red-flagged. Any more trouble, and she could be kicked out."

"I'm glad I was there. I taught for a while and hated the teasing and the bullies." I thought about the emotional pain I'd witnessed and the hurt students who'd shared their stories in subdued voices, tears running down their cheeks.

"Kids can be cruel." Daniel leaned down and pulled out another tray, his long ponytail swinging over his shoulder.

"What I've seen so far of Allie is she's a sweet and loyal kid." I hesitated. I didn't know Daniel well. Asking questions about his personal life felt awkward, but maybe I could help. "What was up with the fighting?"

Daniel didn't look at me. He put the cheese platter on the second tray. "My wife left us. Didn't say a word to Allie. Just wasn't there one morning."

I stopped arranging crackers. "How could a mother do that to her child?"

"She was never a mother, other than in the biological sense. Wanted as little to do with Allie as possible." Daniel glanced at me. Pain filled his eyes. "Allie could never understand why Pam didn't treat her like the other moms she knew."

"Good thing she has you." Tears threatened to well up. "You obviously love her deeply."

"I do." Daniel picked a knife from the holder and put it next to the cheese. "We make a good team. It hurt when Pam left, but I believe it was for the best."

We finished putting together the trays in companionable silence and carried them to the conference room.

"If there's anything else you need, let me know." Daniel gave me a wave good-bye.

Attractive man and devoted father. What would make a woman leave someone like that? My ex only cared for himself and his immediate needs.

I shook off the past and surveyed the room, feeling ready for the silver-haired crime busters.

The Sentinels knew how to organize themselves, so I headed to the lounge area to check on the guests.

In the parlor, Andy was writing at a desk tucked in the corner. "Hey, Kelly, how's it going?"

"Fine, thanks." Now was my chance to question him about where he was this afternoon when I was attacked. "How did your visit go with the cheese makers?"

"Lots of luscious tastes. I'm making notes while they're still imprinted on my taste buds."

"Phil mentioned they changed the time on you to one and the two of you had to cancel your lunch date. Too bad." Would he corroborate the information?

"Yeah. They had to juggle some appointments." He put his pen down and stretched. "It's okay. Phil and I will catch each other another time."

"Good luck with your notes." I left for the conference room.

Check him off as a shoving suspect for now. If I needed to, I could figure out a way to confirm his meeting.

The Sentinels were filling their plates when I returned. A stout woman in a drab olive uniform sat with her back to the door. A California Department of Fish and Game patch was emblazoned on one sleeve. She turned as I entered, pushed her chair back and stood, holding out a hand in introduction. Her calloused palm scraped against mine as we shook.

"Fran Cartwright. Pleased to meet you."

"Kelly Jackson, executive administrator with Resorts International."

"Thanks for arranging the room on such short notice," the Professor said and smiled.

"And thank you for the treats," said Mary in her soft voice.

"You're welcome."

Mary had a plastic container next to her. What confection was yet to come?

The Professor said, "Fran, we really appreciate your prompt response."

"No problem." She sat back down and withdrew a small notebook and pen from her pocket. "I hear you have some exciting news."

I pulled out a chair and sat next to the warden.

The Professor's pen spun in his fingers at an alarming rate. A helicopter ready for liftoff.

"We crack code." Ivan's chest appeared to expand a couple of inches.

Fran shifted in her chair, leather belt creaking. "Professor, you said you had evidence of a good-sized abalone poaching ring."

He reached for the envelope labeled Jerry and Joey on the table and pulled out the papers I'd given him. "It's a list of dates, times, and some notes. They're written in the code the Navajos used in World War II. *TSA-ZHIN* means 'reef' and *GAH-GHIL-KEID* stands for 'ridge.' We've never used the Navajo language in our investigations. However, we decided to use abbreviations and as few words as possible during our last case, to expedite our reports. We made a list we all used. 'Reef' and 'ridge' refer to Agate Beach and Crystal Bay. Once we got the key words, the dates and times fell into place." He set the papers on the table.

"Bob usually kept me in the loop, but I didn't know about this." Fran reached for the notes.

Rudy stood and leaned over the table. He stabbed at a place on the page with his finger.

I craned my neck to see what he was pointing at and saw *4LS* above his jagged fingernail.

"Means four large sacks," he beamed, "of abalone."

"A phrase on one of the pages translated to 'regulate schedule.' The words are not an exact match, but we think it meant regular schedule," said the Professor. "That makes this an ongoing operation."

"These are clipboard notes," Gertie piped up. "There are creases along the top edge. Bob carried them on the front seat of the pickup, along with his schedule for the day."

"The clipboard." Mary's brown eyes stared out from her Pillsbury Doughboy face. A white, fluffy coconut bar halted on its path to its demise as Mary's hand stopped. "Where's Bob's clipboard?"

Chapter 14

"Bob brought the clipboard in with him when he was done for the day," Rudy volunteered.

"I'll go search for it while you fill Warden Cartwright in on the details," I said.

"Fran will do. We're casual in Redwood Cove," the officer said.

"Got it. Same applies to me. Please call me Kelly." I frowned. "Professor, you said this might be why Bob was killed. Going from stealing mollusks to murder seems like a big leap."

"I can help with that," Fran said. "Our last bust netted one hundred sixty-six abalone. On the black market that's about sixteen thousand dollars. We caught them as they were getting ready to harvest more."

"Wow!" I exclaimed. "That's a lot of money. I had no idea they could be worth so much."

"Most end up in San Francisco. Some to be eaten as a delicacy, others to be dried and shipped to China and put on a shelf as a magic cure." She gave a snort of derision and leaned back, running thick fingers through cropped salt-and-pepper hair. "We seized two vehicles and six thousand in cash, as well."

The Professor handed Fran several typed pages of information. "We're not done yet, but we felt we had enough to get in touch with you."

"We've heard rumors of a large, organized ring operating in the area." Fran flipped through the papers. "I see the top page is from a few days ago and the bottom one is almost twelve weeks ago."

"We deciphered the top two pages and the bottom two first," Gertie said. "We thought it might give us a time span."

"Clever." Fran gazed at the intent faces. "It was the community's lucky day when you created the Silver Sentinels."

Broad smiles greeted the compliment.

I got up to search for the clipboard.

"Honey," Mary said to me, "before you go, take one of these." She pushed a Tupperware container across the table.

I noticed some white coconutty things. "Thanks, Mary. I'll grab one when I get back. They look tasty." *Sweet* described Mary in more ways than one.

I left them in deep discussion. A quick check of the work area next to the kitchen revealed nothing. The clipboard hadn't been in the office when I went through everything. Taking the key to the company pickup from its peg near the door and a navy blue loaner fleece sporting the company logo in artful gold lettering, I stepped outside. A cold ocean breeze slapped my face, causing my eyes to water and a shiver to run through me. I quickly put on the jacket, zipping it against the wind.

My boots crunched against the gravel as I walked to the small, red Toyota pickup parked against a fence behind the inn. Peering in the driver's window, I didn't see the clipboard. I unlocked the door and searched under and behind the driver's seat. I sat behind the wheel and reached down between the seats. Nothing.

A metal clip protruding from under the passenger's seat caught my eye. I leaned down and grabbed the edge of what turned out to be the missing item. On top was the sought-after day's schedule and a to-do list. It was followed by the previous two days. Three pages of coded notes were on the bottom of the stack.

Great. These papers would tell us what Bob was doing the day he died. I studied the top page. Suzie's name appeared at eleven. Redwood Ranch was at twelve thirty, and Javier at two completed the day. Helen might know what the last two were about.

I grabbed the door handle and paused for a moment as the fragrance of Old Spice filled my mind with memories. Grandpa wore it, and I pictured him in his rocker. His straw cowboy hat jammed on his head, the brim tightly curled with a sweat-stained hatband. The one Mom had thrown out over and over only to have him dig it out each time.

"It's a dude ranch and a working ranch," he'd protested. "This is my working hat."

Grandpa. When Jezebel, my scheming pony, figured a way to ditch me, he was always right there. If I fell off, he picked me up and put me right back in the saddle. If Jez wouldn't let me catch her, he showed me how. Always teaching. Always guiding. Always a great listener when times were tough. I missed him. And the rest of the family. I leaned my forehead on the steering wheel. Why couldn't I be content working at home? Had I done the right thing taking this job? And now, here I was helping investigate a possible murder. Where was that going to lead?

I sat up in the seat and spied a cup half-full of a dark liquid in the coffee holder. A scum had formed on top. The faces of two young boys in a magnetic frame attached to the dashboard grinned at me. Jerry and Joey? The grandkids? For a moment, I felt Bob was next to me, smiling back at his grandchildren, savoring a cup of freshly ground coffee. Then he vanished as the memory of his death four days earlier hit me.

I leaned back, inhaling the musky cologne, looking at the pictures. Those kids would grow up without their grandfather. Robbed of a special relationship. Why? Because of someone's greed? Fear? Anger? Emotion swept through me, and I smacked the steering wheel with my palm. Whoever killed this man, I wanted the person caught.

A tentative knock sounded on the pickup's window. Wide-eyed, Tommy stared at me, deep lines creasing his forehead. I opened the door.

"Miss Kelly, are you okay?"

"I'm fine, Tommy." I managed a smile. "Thanks for asking."

The frown fled from his face. "Oh good."

"How was school today?"

"Fun. We did a neat science experiment."

I regarded the ever-present basset hound. "Tommy, what on earth is that equipment you have on Fred?"

The dog was wearing an intricate harness of cotton webbing held together with Velcro strips. Tommy held long loops of lightweight cord in his hand. Pink flags sprouted out of his pockets.

"Allie and I are training him to track. She's putting scent out in the field. Gotta go." He was off.

I grabbed the clipboard and returned to the Sentinels. They were like puppies waiting for a cookie. The Professor's fingers twitched in anticipation when he saw what I was carrying.

"I don't understand the need for a code." I pulled the schedules off and handed Bob's notes to the Professor.

"He didn't want anyone to know what he was doing." The Professor scanned the new find.

"Bob seemed worried for weeks." Mary sighed.

"When we asked if anything was wrong," the Professor said, "he replied it, whatever it was, would soon be over."

"We pressed him to tell us," Gertie added, "but he wouldn't."

"He apologized for having said anything and asked us to forget it." Rudy stared at the table. "We reluctantly respected his wishes."

"We want to help, but no." Ivan's large scarred hands gripped the table.

Fran frowned. "Why didn't he want to involve you? You've worked together before."

"He clucked after us like a mother hen when we were on a case," Gertie said. "Maybe he felt this one was too dangerous."

"If these notes are accurate, this group is making a ton of money. They make the bust I told you about look like peanuts." Fran paused. "It's enough to murder for. I can see why Bob might've been worried."

"Or maybe someone we know," Ivan added, his volume like a speaker with the control stuck on loud.

"What do you mean?" I asked.

The Professor's face appeared to age as he talked. "The only two reasons we could think of that would cause Bob to keep what was happening a secret were either a high level of danger or that it involved someone we knew."

"But I still don't understand. People didn't have access to the clipboard, so why the code?" I questioned.

"Those were his working papers," the Professor said. "They were with him constantly, and he consulted them during his appointments. People he visited might have had an opportunity to see something."

Mary wiped a white curl of coconut off her lip. "He left them in the workroom or his office when he was in during the day."

I thought for a moment. "So Bob could've found out who the poacher was and didn't want the person to discover what he knew." I paused.

The Sentinels nodded, no bright eyes or smiles among them.

A cold jet of realization hit me. "It could even be someone at the inn."

Chapter 15

An invisible elephant stampeded into the room and plopped its tonnage in the midst of the group.

The Sentinels shot furtive glances at each other. Someone amongst them? An acquaintance? Worse yet, a friend? No one wanted to open the door to let the beastly thoughts out. The silence lengthened.

"There are a lot of unanswered questions. Maybe they'll get addressed as these notes are deciphered." Fran stood.

The movement dissipated the tension.

"We'll devote all our energy to this as soon as possible," the Professor said.

"Thanks. We have a couple of guys in custody for poaching. What you've given me is enough to ask some questions. Maybe they'll be interested in making a deal. Less jail time in exchange for some names."

I stood, as well. "It was a pleasure to meet you, Fran."

"Same here. I appreciate your help with the meeting and finding the clipboard."

"No one else is scheduled for the room," I told the group. "You're welcome to stay here as long as you like."

I left amidst a chorus of thanks and headed for the kitchen. My watch said it was close to six. Did I really want to go listen to music with Suzie? Doing that seemed a million miles away from where my head was—on murder and a major crime—and not where my time should be spent. But what could I do? I didn't feel I was in a position to add anything to the Sentinels' quest. Fish and Game was handling the abalone end. I had Bob's last day of appointments. I could follow up on those, but that would have to wait until tomorrow when I could reach people at work.

The phone rang. "Hello, Redwood Cove Bed-and-Breakfast, Kelly Jackson speaking. How can I help you?"

"Hi!" Suzie's voice danced over the line. "Are we on for tonight?"

"I don't know, Suzie, I have a lot to catch up on here."

"C'mon. Just for a while." She laughed. "The guys are all going, and they might get Phil to do his Zorba routine."

I paused. The guys—Phil, Andy, and Jason. People who stayed at the inn or came over on a regular basis. I knew what Andy had said about his day and Phil's during the time the BlackBerry was taken. I didn't know Jason's whereabouts. Maybe I could learn something.

"Okay. I'll come for a bit."

"Great. How about in half an hour?"

"That works."

"See you then." Suzie hung up.

Fran had said most of the abalone went to the Bay Area. All the men I wondered about had ties there. What better time to sneak a few questions in than as they ate, drank, and listened to music?

"Hi, Kelly." Helen came in and grabbed a prepared cheese platter from the refrigerator and put it on the counter. "Anything I can help you with?"

"No thanks." I read the labels—Boerenkaas, Ewehoria, Morbier—and laughed. "The cheese world has its own language. These names seem like they're from another planet."

"Bob always let Andy select the cheese. To be an expert like him is like being . . . a race car driver. He's a specialist with a lot of training and experience. Bob knew when to delegate." Helen shook her head and let out a deep sigh as she removed the plastic wrap. "A good man. What a loss."

"I wish I could've known him." I put a hand on Helen's shoulder. "I'm going to meet Suzie and have a bite to eat at Noah's Place. If you need me, call my cell phone."

"It's nice you two have hit it off so well." Helen picked up the tray. "The locals are a tight group. Someone new to the area can be very lonely here."

"I enjoy her company." I opened the door for Helen as she made her way to the parlor. "I'll see you later."

Helen smiled and disappeared down the hall.

Going to my room, I exchanged the company fleece for a light blue one trimmed in black piping. I put the appointment schedule in the folder marked BOB PHILLIPS and grabbed my pack. The walk to Noah's Place was short, but the cold, fog-laden wind pierced my jacket, and I shivered.

I opened the door to Noah's Place, and the aroma of pizza dough, mingled with Italian spices, tomato sauce, and sausage, bombarded me in a blast of warm air. The silence of the walk exploded into the sounds of laughter and friends calling out to each other. I jostled my way past the counter, spotted Suzie at a small table against the wall, and waved a greeting.

"Good work finding a table." I sat.

"I left right after we talked. I know what it's like." Suzie handed me a menu. "We should order before it gets more crowded."

"Good idea." I scanned the menu. "I'm going to have the lentil and tomato soup."

"Sounds good to me, too. What would you like to drink?"

"Sparkling water. Phil took me on a flight of wines today." I rolled my eyes.

"Welcome to Mendocino wine country." Suzie left to place our order.

I glanced around the room and spotted "the guys" pulling slices from a large pizza. Strings of melted cheese dripped down the sides of the pieces. Green and brown beer bottles littered their table. Several musicians tested their instruments. A couple of tables over, Charlie Chan chatted with several young men with long hair and wool caps. Charlie could've overheard me talking to Suzie after Helen told me about the BlackBerry. He had connections in San Francisco, as well.

Suzie returned. "Katey'll bring our food in a few minutes." She placed a Calistoga in front of me and a glass of red wine at her place and sat down.

"Thanks." I took a long, welcome sip of cold, tingling water.

"Hey, Suz, how's it going?" A young man with shoulder-length hair, wearing an Oakland A's baseball cap, came over and gave her a quick hug.

"Fine. Meet my new friend, Kelly Jackson. Kelly, this is George Davidson. He helps with some of the meal preparation at the hotel."

"Glad to meet you," I said.

"Same here," he responded.

The two engaged in an animated conversation, catching up on local news.

I looked back at Charlie and his group. He clapped one of the men on the shoulder, stood, then headed in our direction, nodding at me as he walked past. Instead of turning to go out, he continued straight and entered the men's room. How could I get a chance to question him? Several minutes passed as I racked my brain for ideas.

The bathroom door opened, and Charlie emerged.

"Hey, Charlie, do you have a minute?" I asked as he started to go by.

He stopped. "Sure, what's up?"

"Did you make a delivery around one thirty today at the inn?"

"Yeah. I was there about that time. Why?"

"Did you see anyone?"

"No." He stared at me. "You ask a lot of questions, Ms. Jackson."

"Please call me Kelly." I reached up and started to touch his sleeve. I thought better of it. "I'm sorry. I didn't mean to be rude. We . . ." I hesitated. Should I mention the BlackBerry? No. "We had something taken, and I was hoping you might have seen someone or something unusual."

"I was there about ten, maybe fifteen minutes, swapping full containers for empties in the back. There were no cars in the delivery area."

"Thanks. I appreciate your help."

"Sure. No problem." And no smile. He made his way back to his friends.

Katey placed two steaming bowls of soup and a tray of crackers in front of us. Suzie's friend George drifted off.

"This is perfect. I'm glad I'm here." I took a spoonful. Any lingering chill from the walk fled as I swallowed the rich mixture.

Suzie tasted the soup. "What's up with Charlie? He didn't seem too happy."

"I asked him some questions about something that occurred at the inn today. I thought he might have some information."

"What happened?" Suzie took a sip of wine and put down her glass.

How much should I tell? The deputy thought the thief was a local. If he was right, it could be one of Suzie's friends, for all I knew. And if people got wind I was asking them questions to figure out if they had an opportunity to steal the BlackBerry, I was dead in the water.

"Business stuff. Nothing important." I grabbed my bottle of water. "When does the band start?"

The band answered by beginning a rousing Cajun tune. Perfect timing.

Suzie and I worked our way through our dinner.

The band did three songs before taking a break. "We are the Road Travelers. Glad to have you here," announced the lead guitarist.

The crowd applauded and whistled.

"We've had a special request." He picked a few familiar notes on his guitar.

I couldn't quite place them.

The crowd screamed and began clapping, following the beat of the guitarist.

People standing in front of the band moved away, leaving a clear area. Phil left his buddies and stepped into the space and began sweeping leg movements I recognized from line dancing. The tempo increased, then suddenly burst into the intense speed of "Zorba the Greek."

The crowd yelled even louder and clapped frantically. Phil swirled and spun. The music ended suddenly. Phil froze. A moment of silence. Then pandemonium.

"What a performance!" I turned to Suzie. "That was fantastic."

"He does it once in a while. It's always a treat."

Phil headed back to his table with a big grin as he wound his way through the crowd. Andy and Jason pounded him on the back. Charlie went over and clinked beer bottles with him.

"It's been fun, but I'm going to call it a night," I said to Suzie. "It's been a long couple of days." Questioning Jason would have to wait.

"I'm sure it has. I'll be in touch tomorrow to see if you need anything."

"Thanks again for everything." I pulled a slender flashlight out of my pocket.

I pushed out the door and hit a wall of cold. Walking hurriedly toward the inn, I promised myself I'd wear my down jacket next time, even if I was in California. Lesson learned.

The night was pitch-black. The row of faces in my mind was bright. Andy, Phil, Jason, Charlie. Like a police lineup, but all the faces were happy and smiling. Did one of them have something to hide? Had the smile been replaced by fear or anger at one time? Had one of them murdered Bob?

Chapter 16

I pulled my keys out of the zippered pocket, unlocked the inn's back door, and flipped on the lights. The warm kitchen was a welcome contrast to the cold night air. The scent of freshly baked bread lingered in the room. I checked for messages on the wall phone and saw none. The only sign of life in the parlor was the crackling fire. Folks were probably out enjoying Redwood Cove's fine restaurants. Time for bed.

Helen came into the kitchen as I was leaving for my room. I stopped when I saw the look on her face. "What's wrong?"

"Tommy. He's gone. I found Fred locked in his bedroom." She wrung her hands, the bones pushing white against the flesh. "He left a note saying he'd forgotten something somewhere and had to go back and find it." Her frightened eyes stared at me. "He never goes anywhere without Fred." Her voice trembled. "Something's wrong."

A chill went down my back. "When was the last time you saw him?"

"He came in and worked on the computer for a little while after you left. Then he jumped up and ran out." Helen clenched her hands together, stilling the nervous wringing. "But he always jumps and runs, so I didn't think anything about it." Tears filled the corners of her eyes.

I went to the computer and moved the mouse, bringing the screen to life, and saw only an empty desktop. I double-clicked the e-mail icon and checked the in-box. Luckily, he hadn't logged out. There were three messages—two related to homework and one from a boy complaining about a teacher.

Helen leaned over me. "Do you see anything?" Her voice quavered.

"No. Let me look in the trash." I opened the folder.

"Here's one from Allie at six twenty. 'I found out something about Bob's death. It's for sure not your fault. Meet me on the headlands behind the visitors' center at seven thirty. I'll be watching for your flashlight, and I'll signal you with mine. Don't bring Fred. He can be noisy sometimes. We need to be quiet for what I have planned.'" Another chill raced down my spine.

"Thank goodness he's with Allie." Helen lunged for the phone and stabbed in numbers. "Daniel, Tommy and Allie are on the headlands. I'm scared. It's dark and . . ." She paused. "Allie's there?"

I stood and moved beside her.

"Oh God," she wailed. "Where's Tommy?" She dropped the phone. It bounced up and down on the curled cord.

I grabbed the receiver.

Helen collapsed in a chair, her head in her hands, sobbing.

"Daniel, it's Kelly. I found an e-mail on Tommy's computer from Allie asking him to meet her on the headlands behind the visitors' center."

"Let me check with her."

Daniel asked Allie if she had sent Tommy an e-mail to meet her. Her answer of no came clearly over the line.

"She says she didn't send anything. Kelly, what's going on?"

"Tommy's missing."

"I'm on my way."

I hung up and turned toward Helen. It was like a tableau. Everything was as it had been—the serving trays on the counter, the coats hanging on their pegs, leashes next to them—but nothing was the same. A little boy gone in the dark of night.

"We've got to find him." Helen stood and started for the door. She turned. "But the area's huge. Where do we start? Who did this?" she cried.

"Helen, we're going to find him."

"How?" Her hopeless look pierced my heart.

"I have a plan. You need to go get Fred." I went over and grabbed a short leash from the wall. "Be sure to hold on to him."

Helen's voice held a spark of hope. "What are you thinking?"

I looked at the tracking harness on the wall. "Fred's going to find him."

Helen yanked the leash from my hand and ran out the door.

I hurried to my room, pulled out my cell phone, and dialed 911.

"All circuits busy," came the automated voice.

I groaned in frustration.

Shoving the phone back in my pocket, I put my down jacket on like I was in a race. Actually, I was in a race . . . a race to save Tommy. I spied my hiking boots and hesitated. It would take a couple of extra minutes, but I wouldn't be of any help to Tommy if I fell and hurt myself. Ripping off my black leather walking shoes, I shoved my feet into the boots, tied the laces in record time, and hurried to the kitchen.

Helen clutched Fred's leash like it was a lifeline. The dog was looking around, deep furrows in his brow. Wondering where Tommy was, I was sure.

Helen wore a lightweight blouse.

I pulled Fred's tracking harness from the wall, reached over and grabbed a company fleece, and shoved it in her arms as I took his leash from her. "You'll need this."

I started to put the gear on Fred. I willed myself to be calm as I figured out the intricate webbing. Fred was our best bet. Finally, I had the harness in place.

I looked up and hesitated. Helen wore flimsy leather flats. "Do you have sturdier shoes?"

"I want to leave now. I want to find my son." Her eyes locked with mine.

"If you fall, you'll only slow down the search."

Helen lunged for Fred's leash. "I want to find my son now."

I pulled the leash back out of her reach. "Okay, Helen. We'll go."

I took a lantern from beside the door and handed it to her. I removed the flashlight from its casing next to the light switch.

I opened the door, and Fred nearly took my arm out of its socket. We ran, reached the visitors' center, and raced behind it. There were several trails going different directions. My face stung as the wind whipped my hair into my cheeks.

"Fred, find Tommy. Where's Tommy?" I commanded the dog.

The dog cast from side to side for a few minutes and then charged down one of the narrow paths. I followed with the leash taut between us, my flashlight bobbing up and down. I slipped in patches of mud left from torrential rains a few days earlier. Helen stumbled along behind me.

We both yelled, "Tommy," over and over. The wind snatched our cries and flung them into oblivion. But not the baying of the hound. The centuries-old sound rang through the night. The hunter coming.

The dog veered off the trail, nose to the ground, and lunged toward the cliff's edge. My throat constricted. He was following Tommy's tracks, which led to a precipice. I struggled to hold the dog back. I heard Helen stagger behind me.

"Tommy," she screamed and started to push past me. I held out my arm and stopped her. I put the beam of the flashlight on her face. Dazed. Frightened.

"Helen, you hold Fred." I shoved the leash into her hands. "You know how important he is to Tommy." Helen's hands closed convulsively on the lead.

The dog fought to get away.

"Fred, sit," I said sternly. Hours of training at the cancer clinic paid off, and he obeyed.

Helen appeared about to faint.

"I think it'll be easier to hold on to him if you kneel down and hold his collar." *And you won't have as far to fall if you pass out.*

"But I have to see if Tommy's down there."

"No. It's too dangerous. The edge might give way. I'm going to do this." I gripped her arm. "Tommy needs you safe."

Helen crouched next to the dog, clinging to him.

I turned toward the cliff. I got down on my stomach and crawled forward, pressing the ground in front of me with my hands. No movement of the soil. When I reached the edge, my flashlight couldn't penetrate the blackness beyond. Waves crashed below. Inching ahead, I peered over the brink, pointing the light straight down. There was a narrow path about six feet below. I swung the beam to the left. The path widened to a small ledge.

The light picked up dirty tennis shoes.

Motionless denim-clad legs.

A deathly pale face.

Tommy.

Chapter 17

"Tommy!" I yelled. "Tommy!" I screamed again, fighting the wind and the roar of the crashing waves.

His head moved. He looked up, blinking in the flashlight beam.

Relief exploded through me. "Are you hurt?"

"Ankle . . . sore . . ." His words floated up.

There was more, but I couldn't hear it. "Don't move! I'm coming to get you."

I pushed back quickly from the edge, turned, and ran to Helen. I knelt down and put my arms around her. "It's Tommy. He's conscious. I think he's okay." I hoped what I told her was true.

Helen clutched me and began sobbing as she struggled to stand.

"You stay here with Fred and watch for Daniel."

"No!" She lurched upward. "I've got to get to him."

"Helen, the track's narrow. It's dangerous." I grabbed her arms.

She tried to pull away. The lantern cast dark shadows around her anxious eyes.

"I'm going. You can be the most help by signaling Daniel and holding on to Fred so he doesn't make the situation worse."

She stopped fighting me. Her coldness seeped through the fleece. Her tense body was like an icicle—hard to the touch and ready to shatter into hundreds of pieces.

"Okay." She started to tremble violently. "Hurry. God, please hurry."

I ran left on the path, seeking a way down. The brush only got higher and thicker on my right. I turned back around and raced past Helen. Her eyes were squeezed shut as she hugged Fred to her side. The trail sloped downward. My flashlight picked up a narrow opening in the bushes, and I pushed myself through it, thorny plants grabbing at my jeans. There was a whisper of a trail.

The path veered left, back toward Tommy. Ghostly fingers of fog curled through the beam of light as if beckoning me to join them. I didn't look into the black void on my right. The boom of waves told me everything I needed to know . . . or didn't want to know. The damp, cold wind pierced my down jacket.

My anxiety raced forward but my feet placed themselves slowly and carefully on the narrow trail. It took a curve to the left. The beam of my light finally caught what I had been seeking—Tommy. Tall grass surrounded him on a small flat bed of earth and rock. I knelt beside him.

"Where are you hurt?" I touched him gently and ran my light over him. He grasped my arm, smudges of dirt on his cheeks and clothes. I leaned in, put my arm around him, and his bony shoulders shook through his light nylon jacket.

"My ankle hurts." He clung tighter. "I lost my flashlight. I was too scared to move."

I wanted to ask him what had happened but, more importantly, I needed to get him out of there.

"Let's get you home." I looked up. A light bobbed at the cliff's edge above. Probably Daniel. I pointed my flashlight in that direction and turned it on and off twice. The bright dot in the distance winked in return.

Tommy started to stand.

"Wait. We can't be sure what shape your ankle's in." I held him in place. "It's dangerous here. You might slip and fall."

Boy, was it ever dangerous. The frantic race to find Tommy had blotted out the reality of the situation. Now that I'd reached him, I realized how close death was. One wrong step or crumbling piece of trail, and we'd fall hundreds of feet to the rugged rocks and crashing ocean below. How were we going to get him out of here?

"Really, I think I can walk."

As if on cue, Daniel appeared. He bent down and placed a hand on the boy's shoulder. "I believe you can do it, too, but let's not take any chances. Besides, I have an important job for you to do."

"What's that?" Tommy asked.

"I won't be able to use the flashlight because I'll be carrying you. I need you to light the path for us so we can both be safe. Do you think you can do that?"

Tommy nodded vigorously.

"Daniel," I hesitated. I didn't want to frighten Tommy, but there wasn't any way I could talk to Daniel privately. "Should one of us go for help? I know you can carry Tommy, but . . ." I looked at the meager trail disappearing into blackness.

"Kelly, I grew up running on these trails. As kids we thought it was fun to challenge each other to race as fast as we could." He shook his head. "Dumb. I know. Somehow we all survived."

I could barely make out his features in the dim light from the moon.

"I know how to navigate these trails." Daniel handed Tommy his flashlight and picked him up as if he were nothing more than a light sack of groceries. "It's important you don't move, Tommy."

"Okay."

Tommy's left hand clutched Daniel's jacket tightly. With his right, he aimed the flashlight on the path ahead.

I followed closely behind, putting my beam with Tommy's. It was the longest shortest walk I'd ever taken. The crashing waves were deafening. One boom after another like a watery Fourth of July. Finally, the path turned away from the ocean and into the brush. Helen was waiting for us when we reached the main trail.

Daniel put Tommy down, and I pulled Fred's leash from Helen's hand as mother and son embraced.

"I'm sorry, Mom." Tears streamed down his face.

"Hush, baby." Helen stroked his hair. "Are you all right?"

"My ankle hurts a little, but that's all, I think."

I took off my down jacket and draped it around Tommy's frail shoulders. I smiled at Daniel in the lantern's feeble glow. "I wanted to do that before, but I was concerned it might make him more awkward to carry."

Fred was baying and pulling toward Tommy, so I let the leash out enough for the hound to touch him with his nose, but not to jump up and knock him over.

"Fred, I'm sorry to you, too." Tommy pulled away from his mom and wrapped his arms around the squirming dog. "I'll never leave you behind again."

Daniel picked Tommy up. "Ready to go home, sport?"

"Yep." Tommy shined the light on the path.

Helen grabbed the lantern and walked at her son's side, her hand never letting go of Tommy's arm.

"I know what we need to have tonight," Daniel said.

"What's that?" Tommy asked.

"Daniel's famous triple chocolate hot chocolate. What do you say to that?"

"Oh boy. I love that." The light wavered for a moment. "With lots of whipped cream?"

"You bet." The light snapped back on the path.

I followed with Fred trotting at my side. We made the last part of the walk in silence.

Daniel stopped at his VW bus. Tommy let go of his jacket, and Daniel helped him down. The boy gingerly placed his left foot on the ground. Daniel opened the side door, and Helen got in. Daniel lifted Tommy up onto the seat. Fred struggled to follow, and Daniel gave him an accommodating lift.

"It's only a couple of blocks," I said. The van was packed. Between Helen clinging to Tommy and Fred's thick, wildly waving tail, it didn't leave much room. The back was full of boxes, and the passenger seat held several books. "I'll walk and meet you there."

"Miss Kelly, here's your jacket." Tommy pulled the jacket off, and Daniel handed it to me. "I'm warm now between Mom and Fred."

My light picked up the worn planks of the boardwalk. Tommy had clearly been lured out to the bluff for some reason. I didn't believe Allie would lie. Was it one of the kids who'd gotten her password and did it as a prank? But Allie and Tommy had planned on changing it this afternoon. Maybe they hadn't gotten it done.

Daniel's van drove by. By the time I got back to the inn, they were in the kitchen inspecting Tommy's ankle. The dirt was washed off his arms. A few small, angry-looking red lines remained.

"I don't think it's anything serious." Daniel tousled his hair. "Time for a shower. We need to see if anything is hiding under the rest of the dirt, then the hot chocolate."

Daniel looked at me. "We talked to Tommy about the e-mail. We told him Allie didn't send it. He doesn't have any idea who could have done it."

Now I could ask the question that had been consuming me. "Tommy, what happened? How did you end up on that ledge where I found you?"

He looked at me and gulped. "Someone shoved me off the path."

Chapter 18

Helen emitted a primal moan as Tommy's words sank in. Her eyes widened with a look of horror mixed with hate. Her lips formed a thin, tight line and her hands balled into fists.

"Who pushed you?" The words were a raspy whisper from Helen's emotion-choked voice.

"I don't know. I didn't see him." Tommy slid off his chair and huddled next to Fred. "At least I think it was a man. I'm not sure."

I hesitated questioning him, but the sooner we knew what happened, the better. Gently I said, "Tommy, tell us from the beginning."

"You already know about the e-mail I thought was from Allie." He took a deep breath and stroked the dog's head. "I went to the headlands, and I saw a light flashing. It disappeared before I reached it." He stopped talking.

"Then what?" I prompted in a soft voice.

"Someone grabbed me from behind and knocked my flashlight out of my hand." His voice quavered. "Then he picked me up. It felt like he was getting ready to throw me over the edge of the cliff. I fought to get away."

Helen's knees began to buckle. I grabbed a kitchen stool and scooted it under her. She sat down hard. I kept an arm on her shoulder in case she began to sway. Her face was pasty white.

"Someone else yelled 'no' and I think pulled at his arm. One of his hands let go of me. I got loose. Then he shoved me. I went over the edge. I grabbed at anything I could find to hold on to and ended up where you found me." He put his arms around the stocky neck of the dog and pushed his face into the mottled fur.

The only sound in the room was the shrill whistle from the teakettle.

I'd been holding my breath. I exhaled. Daniel seemed frozen in place like a bronze statue. Helen clutched the counter, her knuckles pressed white against her skin.

Daniel turned off the stove, and the shrieking became a hiss then died away.

Tommy sat up. "I heard arguing above, but it stopped when I heard Fred's baying."

"What did they say?" I asked.

"I couldn't hear much. The wind was really loud." Tommy tugged on one of Fred's ears. "I heard the words *murder* and *accident*." He buried his face in the hound's thick neck. "I don't know who they were," he mumbled. "Sorry."

"There's nothing to be sorry about." I got on my knees beside him and gave him a hug. "Do you have any idea why someone would want to hurt you?"

He shook his head, chewing on his bottom lip.

I got to my feet.

Color began to return to Helen's face. She released her death grip on the counter, stood, and went to Tommy. She held out her hand. "Come on. Let's get you in the shower."

Tommy grasped her hand. Helen pulled him up and wrapped her arms around him. She held him against her, rocking him back and forth. She let him go at last, took his hand, and they walked out. Fred stumbled sleepily after them.

Daniel and I looked at each other. No words came. Someone had tried to kill a little boy. Icy fingers of fear clutched my heart.

"I need to call nine-one-one." I went to the phone.

Daniel took the teakettle off the stove and poured steaming water into a red mug. A deep frown marred his smooth forehead as he opened the cupboard and pulled out a can of cocoa. He poured milk into a saucepan and turned on the burner.

This time I got Dispatch. "I want to report an attempted murder."

"Does the person need medical attention?"

"No." Thank goodness.

"Who was the intended victim?"

"Tommy Rogers, a little boy." Almost murdered.

"And your name?"

"Kelly Jackson." A name they must be getting to know.

"What happened?"

"Someone shoved him off a path." With certain death waiting in the ocean below.

"Where did it happen?"

"The headlands behind the visitors' center." On a cliff.

"Where is he now?"

"At Redwood Cove Bed-and-Breakfast." With all of us watching over him.

"I'll send an officer right out."

I hung up. With a jolt, I realized we weren't all watching over him. He and Helen were by themselves.

I walked over to Daniel. "Do you think there's any danger to Helen or Tommy now?" I looked at him. "They're alone in that little cottage."

He pulled a tea bag out of the cup, dropped it in the sink, and turned off the heating milk. "Time for Helen's tea." He headed for the door. "I'll stay there until they're ready to come back."

"Thanks." Now it was my turn to sit down with a thud. What was going on? Why had someone tried to kill Tommy?

I stretched my back and groaned. Time to call Corrigan. I went to the wall, picked up the portable phone, and entered his number.

"Hello. Corrigan here."

"Hi, Michael. It's Kelly." I took a deep breath. "There's been an incident."

"What happened?"

I recounted the story and waited as the silence on the other end of the line lengthened.

"I'm glad to hear the boy's okay." He sighed. "I'm sending Scott out. He'll get there as soon as he can."

I didn't argue. I knew the company rules. Any serious incident called for a second manager on site. I had talked him out of it once. This time I wasn't going to try.

"How soon do you think he'll get here?"

"Probably sometime tomorrow afternoon or early evening."

That gave me some time to try to sort things out on my own. Once Scott got here, that might not be so easy.

"I'll stop by the inn as soon as I get in on Saturday. It'll be helpful to me to have Scott there, as well."

A knock sounded on the front door. "There's someone here. Probably the deputy."

"See you Saturday then. And . . . Kelly, be careful."

"Right. 'Bye."

Be careful. But who was the threat? Who was I supposed to be careful around?

I went to the front door and peeked through the small hole. Deputy Sheriff Bill Stanton stood under the porch's light.

"Good evening, Deputy Stanton." I swung the door wide. "Please come in."

"Evenin', ma'am." He moved his six-foot-plus frame with grace through the opening. "I hear something else has happened. This time an attempted murder?"

Did I detect a hint of skepticism?

"Yes. Someone tried to kill Tommy." I walked ahead of him to the kitchen, biting my tongue in frustration. Mom's voice spoke to me, reminding me to think before speaking, especially when I was mad.

Memories of Mom's words corralled the rush of anger by the time I reached the workroom. I turned to the deputy sheriff. "Tommy's showering. Daniel and Helen will bring him over here when he's done." I took a deep breath. "Would you like some coffee or tea?" *Be polite, Kelly, be polite.*

"No thanks." The deputy removed his hat and placed it on a nearby chair. "What happened?" He pulled a notebook from his pocket and leaned against the counter.

I told the story. I was amazed to see this bulk of a man making tiny notes in a miniscule pocket notebook. It must be something they taught them at the police academy.

He snapped the book closed and viewed me with weary eyes. "Sounds like a close call."

"Yes. I agree." I had a feeling it was linked to Bob's death, but I didn't know how. Murder and an attempted murder. Throw in robbery and poaching. They had to be connected.

The back door opened and a scrubbed, clean Tommy entered, his face flushed from the hot shower. Helen held his hand. Fred lumbered behind, and Daniel brought up the rear. Tommy stopped when he saw the deputy.

"Hi, Tommy." The officer smiled. "I'm Deputy Sheriff Stanton."

It was the first time I'd seen the deputy be anything but stern and, in my opinion, uncooperative. This was a nice change.

"I hear you've had quite an adventure." He patted the stool beside him. "Have a seat. I'd like to hear about it."

"Deputy Stanton, do you need to do this now?" Helen pulled Tommy closer to her. "Can't it wait until tomorrow?"

"Sorry, Mrs. Rogers. It's important I get as much information now as I can while it's still fresh in his mind." He looked at Tommy. "Do you watch police shows on television?"

The boy nodded. "Yeah."

"Okay, then. We're going to act like we're on TV."

Tommy looked at him with interest. I was beginning to see another side to the deputy.

"Hop up here on this seat, and I'll ask you questions like they do on television."

Tommy clambered onto the stool.

The deputy extended his hand. "My name is Deputy Sheriff Bill Stanton." His voice had a melodramatic ring to it.

Tommy's small hand disappeared in Stanton's large one.

He released Tommy's hand, opened his notepad, and straightened up. "What's your name, young man?"

Tommy straightened up, too. "Tommy Rogers, sir."

"I have some questions to ask you." The deputy frowned theatrically.

"Shoot."

For some reason, I wished Tommy hadn't used that word.

Daniel interrupted from the kitchen. "Before you get started, I think our witness could use some hot chocolate for this interrogation." The chocolate's rich, sweet scent permeated the room. He poured steaming liquid into a mug decorated with frolicking dogs and put a large spoonful of fresh whipped cream on top. He garnished it with curls of chocolate. "Time for triple hot chocolate." He handed the boy the mug.

Tommy's eyes grew big as he accepted the cup with two hands. He took a sip and acquired a white, pencil-thin moustache. "Does it have the chocolate chips at the bottom?"

"You bet. It wouldn't be triple hot chocolate without those."

"Deputy Stanton, would you like some hot chocolate?" Daniel asked.

"You know, don't mind if I do."

What? The gruff deputy drinking hot chocolate? No way.

"Whipped cream?" Daniel asked.

"No. I'll pass on that."

"That's the best part." Tommy now wore a full white moustache. He licked cream from his lips.

Stanton laughed. "If I was your age, I'd have it. Got to watch the calories these days."

Between the hot chocolate and the laugh, the tension in the room evaporated. Who would've thought the big guy could be so sensitive.

"Kelly, chocolate?" Daniel asked.

"No, thanks."

"So, Tommy, tell me what happened," the deputy sheriff said.

Tommy rattled away.

I heard nothing new.

The boy's eyes went to half-mast and then closed.

The deputy stood. "Tommy, I'll come back in the morning. I don't want you to go to school tomorrow."

"Gee, thanks." Tommy was now wide awake.

"You still have to do your homework and make up the classwork you miss," Deputy Sheriff Stanton said in a stern voice.

Tommy nodded vigorously.

"And I want you to stay with your mom, Daniel, or Kelly at all times. Understand?"

Tommy nodded again.

The deputy looked from me to Daniel. "Is that okay with you two?"

We agreed in unison.

I'd been thinking about the coming night during the questioning. "Helen, I think you, Tommy, and Fred should stay in the inn tonight. The Magnolia Room is open. It has two double beds."

Helen's haggard eyes spoke their gratitude. "Thanks."

Stanton turned to Daniel. "I'd like to see where the incident took place tonight. Can you take me there?"

"No problem. Let me help them get their things, and then I'll show you where it happened."

I picked up Tommy's empty cup and put it in the sink. Daniel went out with Helen, Tommy, and the ever-present Fred.

"Ms. Jackson," the deputy sheriff said.

"Yes?"

"This opens a whole new door to what's been happening here." He paused. "You could be right about Bob."

I tried really hard to keep the I-told-you-so look off my face.

Chapter 19

The alarm clock's incessant buzz snapped me out of a fitful sleep. I welcomed the intrusion; it had been a long night. I reached over and punched the button, stretched, and winced as bruises reminded me of their presence. The events of last night poured into my mind. I closed my eyes, and visions of a dirt-covered Tommy lying on a cliff flashed on my mental television. Time to get up. I swung my legs over the side of the bed and stood. I needed coffee. Strong coffee.

Walking into the suite's living area, I slid the divider to the sunroom back. The morning sun hadn't made the black beast of night flee yet. I was completely exposed to anyone who might be outside while I could see nothing. I quickly closed the partition.

I went through the steps of coffee prep while my mind wrestled with questions. Who tried to kill Tommy? What did the boy know? Had he seen something? Who was the second person on the cliff? Was this recent attack connected to the BlackBerry theft and Bob's death?

Only questions. No answers. I had to make a plan.

My shower was a fast one. I did my daily makeup routine on autopilot. Dressed, I sat and began jotting ideas. I needed to question Tommy about Allie changing her password. When did she do it? Who was present? I wanted him to go through the last couple of days again. I believed him when he said he didn't know any reason why someone would want to hurt him, but there had to be something. I needed to explore at the site of the incident. We had Bob's schedule. I would read it over and talk to the most recent people he'd seen. I'd check with the Sentinels and see if they'd discovered anything new.

I put the pen down, relieved I now had a direction.

Scott. What was I going to do about him? Would he take over? He was higher up in the organization and could do that. Then there was the growing attraction I'd been feeling. He'd been popping into my mind more and more. The idea of risking another relationship made me as cold as a winter night in Wyoming.

I needed to put thoughts of him in a mental box right now. I had other things to deal with. Among them, managing the inn.

I went to the kitchen.

Helen was busy with the breakfast baskets.

"Did you and Tommy sleep okay last night?"

"He did." Her voice was raspy from shouting the night before. She arranged raspberry croissants on a plate and garnished them with fresh berries. "He's still asleep." She nodded toward a blanket-covered bundle in a large overstuffed chair. Fred snored on the floor near him. Helen wrapped the plate with plastic wrap. "Little sleep for me."

It showed. Her face was tight and drawn. The sunken areas under her eyes were blue-black splotches.

"I'll have Daniel check the windows and doors of your cottage to be sure the locks are secure. Then I'm having an alarm system put in." I paused. "Even if this hadn't happened, I think it's a good idea."

"Thanks. I appreciate it." Helen wiped her hands on a blue-checkered towel. Her shoulders slumped.

She's carrying their world—Tommy's and hers—on that gaunt frame. It must be tough. "Let me help you."

We completed the food preparation and packed the baskets. The blanket began to move and make noise.

"I'll deliver these so you can stay with Tommy. After that, I'm going for a short walk."

"Kelly, thanks once again."

After the baskets were placed, I shrugged into my jacket, unbolted the front door, and headed for the scene of last night's attack. The rising sun was hidden in the hills behind me, but it had pushed the blackness away to a drab, gray dawn. The tent poles for tomorrow's festival were piled on one side of the expansive front lawn. They looked like a pile of giant bones in the sparse morning light.

I reached the spot in less than ten minutes. Fresh soil had been turned over where Tommy had pulled grass out by the roots, trying to stop his fall. I leaned over, peered below, and shuddered. Huge rocks and crashing waves were hundreds of feet below, and the drop was only a few feet beyond the ledge where I'd found him.

A flush of anger rushed through me. I clenched my fists. I'd get this person. If it was the last thing I did, I'd get him. I looked around, and it hit me why the attacker chose this spot. Aged, gnarled pines, bent by years of relentless winds, grew a few feet away in a huddled bunch. Scanning the bluff, I spotted no other stand of trees. The perfect place to hide. That answered one question—why this place on the cliff.

I walked slowly back to the inn. A collection of locals occupied a corner near a coffeehouse. Some dogs lounged on the boardwalk, while others greeted their doggie friends. Rusted, dusty pickups raised high on oversized tires sat nearby. A Great Dane mix wagged his tail at me and looked with hopeful eyes for a friendly pat, or better yet, a cookie. His owner talked with a bleary-eyed individual clasping a large mug with both hands.

"May I pet your dog?"

A denim-clad young man held the rope tied to the enormous tan dog's collar. "Sure. He's always up for attention." He went back to conversing with his friend.

I rubbed the dog's ears as he leaned into me. As I scratched his side, the dog's owner said to the man next to him, "Did you hear about what happened on the headlands last night?"

"No." His friend had the look of a long night—face unshaven, red eyes squinting into the distance.

"Someone tried to off the kid that lives at Redwood Cove B&B. You know, the little scrawny one that's with the funny-looking dog all the time."

"You're kiddin'." The man's eyes opened a fraction of an inch wider.

"Nope. Jake just told me." He took a sip of coffee. "Tried to toss him off the cliff."

"No!" Eyes a millimeter wider.

They stopped talking and contemplated their coffee cups.

Oh my gosh. I couldn't believe what I was hearing. How did they know this? I had to find out. How could I keep them talking? Maybe feeding them some new information they could impress their friends with would do the trick. Something that wouldn't jeopardize the case.

"Thanks for letting me pet your dog. He's a sweetie. I couldn't help but overhear what you were saying. I was there last night."

The man studied me. Wary. Conflicted. Probably wanted to learn more, but reluctant to talk to an outsider.

"What d'ya mean you were there?"

"I'm interim manager at the B&B. As I'm sure you know, the former manager, Bob Phillips, died recently."

Both men nodded, looking somber.

The dog put his head in his master's lap.

The man scratched the dog's furry neck. "We heard about someone being sent to take over."

"When Tommy went missing, I helped search for him."

The man whom I hoped to trade information with inspected the contents of his cup.

"Rumor has it the hound tracked him." He looked at me expectantly.

"Yes. His dog found him." Now my turn. "How do you know what happened?"

"There's a communication system here that's like a wildfire." The dog's owner exchanged furtive glances with his friend then looked back at me. "If something happens around here, everyone in town knows in half an hour, an hour max." He tossed back his last bit of coffee. "One of my friends told me. Don't know how he found out."

"Thanks." I headed back to the inn.

Wonderful. The whole town already knew. There wouldn't be any covert questioning without people knowing where I was headed.

I entered the workroom just as Andy and Phil burst in. Tommy was eating cereal, while Helen washed dishes.

"Tommy, how are you? I heard about your terrible experience," Phil said.

"Oh my. Oh my," was the best Andy could produce.

Tommy's face paled.

Helen stopped washing dishes and turned to the men. "Andy and Phil, I think Tommy . . ."

A knock on the door, a turn of the handle, and there was Jason.

He rushed in. "My boy, are you okay? I came over as fast as I could when I heard."

Tommy was as still as a statue.

As well-intentioned as the men were, Tommy's eyes were getting bigger by the minute.

"Guys, your concern is really touching, but I think we should go in the parlor and talk," I said.

A look of understanding settled on Phil's face. "Good idea." He grabbed Andy's arm and started for the front of the building.

I touched Jason's shoulder and nodded toward the front of the house.

"I made this for you." Jason gave Tommy a cupcake with chocolate frosting, colorful sprinkles, and TOMMY written in purple icing on top.

"Oh boy. Cool." He began to look like a normal little kid again, his eyes devouring the decorated treat, color returning to his face.

"If there's anything we can do to help either of you," Phil said over his shoulder to Helen, "please let us know."

"That's very kind," Helen said.

"Mr. Phil?"

"Yes, Tommy?" The wine merchant turned back toward him.

"I have to stay home today from school. I'm working on a Greek mythology project. Could you help me with that?"

He beamed. "Absolutely."

"We can't ask you to do that," Helen said. "I know you have work to do."

Phil puffed out his chest and threw back his head. "I'd be honored to help him understand the stories of my culture. Too many times people get it all wrong." He looked at Tommy. "I'll be back in a little bit, and we can talk about gods, and goddesses, and Greece, and . . ." He stopped as he saw my arched eyebrows.

I shooed the guys into the front room. "How on earth did all of you find out about what happened?"

"The delivery man at the hotel told me," Jason said.

Andy, who'd recovered the power of speech, said, "The newspaper boy, and I told Phil."

Another question to answer. Who first told what happened? Certainly not the murderer. Or could it be?

"I think it's best if we let Tommy try to have as normal a day as possible." I looked at each of them. "That means not talking about what happened."

The three men nodded.

"Why don't you tell me what you know? I'm curious to see whether it's accurate and if there is anything you know that I don't," I said.

They had it all. Every detail. There weren't that many people who knew about last night—Tommy, Helen, Daniel, the deputy sheriff, me, the attacker, and whoever stopped him.

"That's what happened." I stood. "Please watch for anything unusual happening around here, and let me know if you hear anything else."

Again the three nodded.

Who was most likely to have told the story? I returned to the work area. Tommy was finishing his cereal and reading the newspaper comics.

"How are you feeling today?" I asked.

"Okay," he mumbled, working on a mouthful of cereal.

"Did you tell anyone about what happened after you talked to Deputy Stanton?"

He nodded. "I texted Allie last night. I knew she'd want to know." He took another spoonful of cereal and went back to reading.

Texted Allie. The whole school probably knew before first period.

Then their parents.

Then their friends.

What about the attacker? Did he know Tommy survived?

Chapter 20

There was a quiet tap on the back door. I spied Rudy's face through the window and waved him in.

"Hi, Rudy," Helen said.

He did a little bow to her and then looked in Tommy's direction. "Good morning to the both of you."

Tommy glanced up and gave him a quick wave.

"Madam Kelly, is okay I help get ready for the festival tomorrow by weeding flowers beds?" He held up a garden trowel.

"That would be wonderful. How nice of you to offer." The plethora of flowers and shrubs could employ an army in a never-ending battle to keep the garden neat.

"I want talk with you about couple of plants. Would work now for you?" His Russian accent was heavier than usual.

"Now's fine." I got up and joined him.

Once outside, Rudy asked, "How is the boy? We heard what happened."

We? Did all the Silver Sentinels know?

"He seems to be doing fine." I looked at him. "How did you find out?"

"Mary's son called her." He shrugged. "She called me. We have phone tree for getting to everyone fast."

Of course. It made sense the Sentinels would have an efficient communication system.

"You said you wanted to talk about a couple of plants."

"Pretend. Wanted to ask about the boy."

"Thanks for helping with the garden."

He nodded and bent down to pick up a small foam kneepad and he walked to the flower bed closest to the tent's skeleton parts. His once-black turtleneck matched his faded, heavy cotton trousers. Rudy dropped the trowel and the pad and then carefully lowered himself to the ground. Kneeling, he began to dig and pull weeds.

I went back into the work area and sat across from Tommy. He was about done with his breakfast. "Yesterday when there was the confrontation with the young thugs, as Allie called them, there was some mention of Allie's e-mail address being used, and you were going to change the password so it didn't happen again."

Tommy nodded. "We talked about a new one as soon as we got back here. We made it Spreckles13." He grinned. "The name of her new kitty and her age."

"Did you tell anyone her new password?"

"No." He looked at me, hurt in his eyes. "I would never do that, Miss Kelly."

"I didn't think you would." I touched his arm. "I'm sorry, Tommy. I had to ask. Someone sent you a phony e-mail, and we have to find out who."

"It's all right." He didn't look at me as he pushed the remaining soggy cereal around in his bowl.

I didn't think it was all right. I didn't want him to feel bad, but I had to know how his attacker had gotten the information.

"Was anyone nearby when you and Allie were discussing the new password?"

"Only grown-ups."

Only. Adults didn't count.

"Do you remember who?"

He cocked his head to the side. "Phil, Andy, and Jason." He pointed a slender finger in the direction of the worktable. "And Daniel was putting food away." He shrugged. "That's all I remember."

"Did Charlie, the water deliveryman, come while you were talking about the password?"

He frowned and then his brow cleared. "Yeah. He changed the bottle next to Allie. She had to move for a few minutes."

All the people I thought could've taken the BlackBerry had an opportunity to hear the two kids. Any of them could've been involved in the attack on Tommy.

I breathed deeply. "Whoever tried to hurt you last night must have had a reason. Let's go over the last few days, starting with yesterday. Think back to what you saw or heard."

Tommy turned to his mom. "Can I eat the cupcake now?"

Helen walked over and rested her hands on his thin shoulders. "May I," she gently corrected him. "Half now, half later."

"Thanks!" He plucked a piece of cupcake and popped it in his mouth.

"So, what did you do yesterday?" I pulled him back to the topic at hand.

"After Allie and I changed her password, I did some homework, then went to the post office for my mom."

"Did you see anyone you know?"

He pinched off another piece of the pastry. "Yeah." He looked at the ceiling, chewing on the cupcake. "The water guy was talking to Andy near the hardware store across from the post office."

"You mean Charlie?"

"Yeah."

Was there some kind of connection between the two of them? Or was it only casual conversation? "Then what?"

"I came home and ate." His face clouded over. "Then I got the e-mail I thought was from Allie."

"Let's go to the day before yesterday," I quickly said. "Start with the evening."

He thought for a moment. "I had dinner, finished my math, watched TV, and went to bed."

"And earlier in the day?"

His face lit up. "Allie and I went to Noah's Place for ice cream. I *love* the banana chocolate fudge."

I laughed. "Sounds good. I'll have to try it."

He began pulling the paper off the cupcake.

"You're doing great, Tommy. Just keep working back through the day."

"I went to the market for Mom." He stopped. The expression on his face closed like a slammed door. "I really need to go do my homework now." He squirmed in his chair. "Can we talk later, Miss Kelly?"

His face had gone pale; his eyes had an owlish look. An expression he'd been wearing a lot lately. But his jaw was clenched. That was new. Tommy, stubborn?

He knew something and wasn't telling. I was torn. Should I keep questioning him or let it be for now? He'd had a tough night. I didn't want to upset him, but someone had tried to kill him. "How about just a little more of the day?" I urged.

"I need to go." He pushed his cupcake away with only a small portion eaten. "Mom, I don't feel like having any more now."

"Okay, sweetheart. I'll wrap it up for you," Helen said. "How was it?"

He lit up like a Christmas tree. "It was cool. There's even pieces of chocolate inside. Jason's cool."

Tommy had plucked pieces from all around the sides, leaving his name intact.

The distinctive rattle of Daniel's bus came closer, and gravel crunched as he parked.

Daniel swung the door open. "Good morning."

"Hi, Daniel. See what Jason made for me." Tommy pointed to the prized treat.

Daniel walked over and peered down. "How great is that? It even has your name on it."

"Yeah. And it has chocolate inside."

"And we know chocolate's good, don't we?"

"We sure do," Tommy said.

Daniel turned to me. "Is there anything in particular you want me to work on today?"

"Yes. I'd like you check out the locks on the doors and windows in Helen's cottage and research what it will take to get an alarm put in."

"I can check the cottage now, if that works for you and Helen." He glanced in Helen's direction.

"That's fine with me," I said.

Helen nodded.

"I need to go home and work on my report." Tommy slid off the stool and headed for the door.

"Tommy," Helen called after him. "Do you remember what Deputy Stanton said last night about one of us being present?"

Tommy stopped. "Yeah. You, Daniel, or Miss Kelly need to be with me. But I'm only going next door to our house."

"Let's follow the policeman's orders." I hoped by making it sound official it would take the sting out of the situation. "We can talk to him about it when he comes this morning. Daniel's working over there, so we'll be doing what the deputy requested."

"Okay." Tommy shrugged. "C'mon, Fred."

The dog pulled himself up and trotted after the boy.

"I'm going to have my work cut out for me keeping up with the dynamic duo." Daniel followed them out the door.

I picked up the remaining dishes on the table and put them in the sink, thinking about what the deputy had asked us to do. Right now we could trust no one.

"Tommy asked Phil to help him with his project," I said.

Helen bent to put a dish in the dishwasher. "He's such a kind man."

"And one of us needs to be there when he's working with Tommy."

She snapped upright. "What do you mean?"

"Deputy Stanton said one of us three was to be there at all times."

Helen shook her head from side to side. "But it's Phil. He wouldn't hurt anyone."

"I don't think he would, either."

Ours eyes locked. Helen's face drained of any remaining color.

"We have no idea who tried to hurt him," I added gently.

"You suspect even people we know?" Her voice quavered.

"I don't think it's about being suspicious of everyone and filling our lives with fear." I searched for the right words. "I think it's about being careful and not making exceptions."

Helen thought for a moment, then nodded. "I understand."

Phil burst into the room, humming. I recognized musical notes from "Never on Sunday."

"Where's my student?" He gave an upward flourish of his right arm. "I'm ready to teach him the real stories about the Greek gods and goddesses."

"He left a few minutes ago to work on it in the cottage. Your timing is perfect."

"Fantastic." Phil left, following in the tracks of Daniel, Tommy, and Fred.

"I'll go over and share with Daniel what we talked about," I said to Helen. "Then we can catch up on tonight's guests."

"Sounds good."

"Helen, the inn's full tonight. I want you and Tommy to stay in my room."

"Oh no. We couldn't do that. That's not right."

I went over and stood next to her. "What's right is for you and Tommy to be safe. I need to be on site, so I can pull a roll-away bed into the small conference room."

"Absolutely not. You can stay in our cottage." She stopped for a moment. "Unless you don't feel safe there."

"I'm not worried about myself. Tommy's the one in danger. I don't want to intrude in your home."

"Fair's fair. If we use your room, I want you to have mine."

"Deal. I'm going to go talk to Daniel now."

A loud knock on the door changed my plans. Stanton stood outside.

"I'll go talk to Daniel." Helen wiped her hands on a dish towel.

Maybe he had some information. Or better yet, maybe they got the guy. "Great."

I opened the door. "Good morning, Deputy Sheriff Stanton."

"Same to you, Ms. Jackson."

"Would you like a cup of coffee?"

"Very much so." He sat on one of the stools and put his hat on another. Deep lines etched his face.

I poured the coffee and handed it to him. "Any news?"

"No. We searched the area and found nothing." He took a sip and stared into the mug. "I came to ask Tommy some more questions."

"Let's go in the study first, and I'll fill you in on what I've found out."

He looked at me quizzically. "Playing detective, are we?"

I knew the heat filling my face ushered in a beet-red blush. Darn. "I'm trying to help figure out what happened . . ." I stammered. "I'm not being a detective . . ." I took a deep breath and willed myself to be calm. "I want to find answers to Bob's death and the attack on Tommy. I have a stake in both. So does the company I work for."

Deputy Stanton chuckled. "Hold on. No reason to get riled up." He took another drink of his coffee. "Anything that helps to find who attacked the little boy is appreciated." He rose. "I look forward to hearing what you know."

We settled ourselves in the inn's office, and I brought him up to speed about Allie's password, how everyone in town seemed to know what happened, what Tommy told me about his activities, and my suspicion he was holding something back.

"Deputy Sheriff Stanton, we have three crimes we're sure of so far—the theft of the BlackBerry and my being shoved, abalone poaching, and the attack on Tommy." I paused. "I really feel the events are connected in some way."

The deputy shrugged. "I'm listening."

"We know Helen, Jason, Andy, Phil, and Daniel were here when the BlackBerry was returned."

The officer nodded.

"Suzie knew about the return because of my conversation on the phone." I paused. "Charlie was in earshot when I talked to Helen."

Deputy Stanton jotted down notes.

"Charlie showed up not long after with a delivery." I drummed my fingers on the desk. "They were all here when the kids changed the password, except for Suzie. She couldn't have e-mailed him. That lets her out of the attack on Tommy and, if the incidents are connected, she didn't steal the BlackBerry." The face of last night's frightened mother flashed through my mind. "And, of course, Helen's not a suspect."

Deputy Stanton shifted in his chair. "If we go with your train of thought, we're considering five possible suspects—Jason, Andy, Phil, Charlie, and Daniel."

No. It couldn't be any of them. I didn't want it to be any of them. I shook my head in disbelief. And Daniel was on the list.

It couldn't be Daniel.

Could it?

Chapter 21

My mind raced through the events of last evening. Relief surged through me. "It couldn't have been Daniel. He didn't have time to get to the headlands to attack Tommy."

"How do you figure?"

"I called him at home. Between the time I talked to him and when we made it to the headlands was about ten minutes, fifteen tops. Fred began baying as soon as we hit the trail. Tommy said the people arguing above him stopped when they heard the dog. Daniel lives too far away to get there that fast."

"Okay. I'll buy that. Daniel's off the hook for the attack on Tommy and if, I repeat if, the two events are related, he didn't steal the Black-Berry."

"That leaves Andy, Phil, Jason, and Charlie." I shook my head. "I can't imagine any of them doing it."

"If criminals looked like crooks, my job would be a piece of cake." He laughed.

The deputy stood and picked up his mug. "Have you seen any of them today?"

I nodded. "All except Charlie. They came to find out how Tommy was doing."

"Do you know where they are now?"

"The last I knew Phil was at the cottage helping Tommy with a report about Greece. Daniel's with them. I don't know about the others."

"I'll go talk to him." Deputy Stanton opened the office door. "And as I said, I want to ask Tommy some more questions."

I grabbed my coffee and followed him out. "You're welcome to use this room."

"Thanks. I might take you up on that."

As we entered the kitchen, Mary fluttered in carrying a wicker basket covered with a red-checkered dish towel.

"Deputy Stanton, Kelly, what perfect timing." She smiled, and her dimples popped into view. "I have something for you." Mary pulled back the cloth, revealing saucer-sized chocolate chip cookies.

The fresh-baked smell triggered my crave button. I'd just eaten, but my taste buds convinced me starvation was close if I didn't eat one of those monster treats dotted with chocolate pieces.

"They're still warm. That's when they're the best." She held the basket out to Deputy Stanton.

"Don't mind if I do." He picked one up and took a bite. "Delicious. Glad I didn't leave earlier."

"Thanks, Deputy." Mary blushed, dimples working overtime.

I didn't try to resist this time. Chocolate chip cookies and coffee together were number one on my list of self-indulgences.

"Ditto what Deputy Stanton said about delicious." I followed the bite of soft cookie with a long sip of coffee. Heaven.

The officer picked up his hat. "Got to go."

"Wait. Take some with you. I know you've had a long night, and you have a lot ahead of you today." Mary placed the basket on the counter.

"I'll get something to put them in." I pulled open a drawer, took out a plastic bag, and handed it to Mary.

She placed six of the oversized cookies in it and handed the baked goods to the deputy.

"Thanks. These'll definitely help me through the day." He put on his hat and headed outside.

I looked through the back door window. He put the cookies in his patrol car and then walked toward the cottage to find Phil and Tommy.

"I thought Tommy and Helen might like something to cheer them up a bit." Mary put the remaining cookies in a bowl on the counter.

"That's thoughtful of you."

"Honey, I noticed the yellow roses in the side yard are in bloom. They're my all-time favorite flower." She pulled a paperback from the side pocket of her purse and held it up. "Would you mind if I sat next to them awhile and read my book?"

The cover depicted a young woman with long blond hair blowing wildly around her and a stern-looking, tanned, well-buffed man watching her.

I smiled. "Stay as long as you like."

Mary took a note from her purse and placed it next to the gift. "I'll come out with you. I want to see how Rudy's doing."

"Rudy's here?" Mary asked in her soft voice, raising her eyebrows.

"Yes. He came over to clean the garden beds for the festival."

"Oh, he's such a sweet man."

As we approached, Rudy stood and dusted off his pants.

"Good morning, dear ladies."

"Hi, Rudy." Mary walked over to a bush exploding with flowers. "These are the ones." She pointed at the magnificent blooms.

A gentle breeze enveloped me in perfumed air. "Their fragrance is wonderful."

Mary settled herself on a nearby bench and opened her book. "Thanks for letting me stay."

"No problem. I'm happy to have you here." And I was. I was becoming fond of this group of senior citizens.

"I'm done for today," Rudy said. "I'll come back in the morning before the festival to do a little more."

I surveyed the newly weeded flower bed. "You did a very nice job, Rudy. Thank you."

"My pleasure." He picked up his kneeling pad and waved good-bye.

I passed the deputy's cruiser as I returned to the kitchen. I glanced down the hallway. The study door was closed. What would Phil have to say?

Had the four stayed at Noah's Place after I left? If so, they were in the clear. It was an easy enough question to ask, but I was a stranger. And this was a very closed community to outsiders.

The phone rang.

"Hello. Redwood Cove Bed-and-Breakfast. Kelly speaking."

"I just heard what happened to Tommy," Suzie's normal cheer lacked in her voice. "Is he okay?"

"He seems to be doing fine. I think staying home from school helped brighten his day."

"Who would do something like this? Is there anything I can do?"

Her questions suddenly gave me an answer—how to get information from the locals.

"Suzie, I have no idea who'd try to hurt Tommy, but I'd like to find out. Will you help me?"

"Of course. What did you have in mind?"

I hesitated. I wanted to know who left Noah's Place right after I did, but that was coming on pretty strong. A local could've pushed Tommy. Maybe even someone Suzie knew. That might be too close to home for her.

"I'd like to find out who was at Noah's Place during the time of the attack on Tommy last night. Those people can be ruled out." I decided to put a positive spin on it. "It's not much, but it's a starting point." I paused. "I'm new here, and I don't think anyone will talk to me about their whereabouts. But they'll talk to you. You're a local. You're one of them."

"Good idea. Can you meet me there at two? We can talk to Noah and see what he knows."

"You bet." I checked my watch. Ten o'clock. "Would eleven this morning work for me to come over and get the keys?"

"Fine. There's a converted garage at the back entrance to the hotel we use for storage. I'll meet you there."

Suzie was the first stop on Bob's list. Maybe there was time to see the other two before the meeting at Noah's Place. I retrieved the list from my room, along with my jacket, and headed for Helen's cottage. Would the people at Redwood Ranch or Javier be able to give me some information to help solve Bob's death? And, if connected, reveal Tommy's attacker? I sure hoped so. Tommy's life was in danger until the police arrested the person.

Chapter 22

I followed the flagstone path to the cottage. The large slabs of stone ranged in color from deep red to slate gray. Bright green moss sprinkled with miniscule white flowers grew between them.

I knocked on the door.

"Who's there?" Helen asked.

Good. She was being cautious. "It's Kelly."

Helen opened the door. "Hi. How can I help you?"

"I have Bob's schedule from the day he fell." No reason to mention the word *murder* after what happened last night. "I'm getting up to speed on what was happening before he died. I'd like to see these people. I thought maybe you could help with directions and background on what Bob was doing at these places."

"Happy to." She signaled me in, and I followed.

On my left in the living area I passed a meadow green couch with yellow pillows placed at each end. They sported a pattern of white daisies with green stems and made a picture-perfect accent. Yellow-and-white-checked gingham curtains with a thin line of green trim carried the colors to the other side of the room. A fireplace built with smooth, round stones occupied the right wall. Windows on both sides of it framed a blue ocean view.

A dining room table was visible at the far end. A short hallway led off to my left with three doors. The bedrooms and the bathroom I'd read about in the company information. Cozy.

"Give me a few minutes," Helen said. "I need to put some flowers in water. I just cut them."

The kitchen alcove was off to the side of the dining area and not visible when I first walked in. A bunch of white calla lilies lay on the counter. Helen put water in a vase and started arranging them.

"Okay." I wandered over to the mantel above the fireplace, where rows of pictures formed a straight line. A black-and-white one showed a young woman in a long black dress with a full skirt, her hair wound up in an elaborate braid on top of her head, a small hat perched on top. Next to her stood a tall man in a vest and slacks. Then came a photo of a young man in a soldier's uniform.

The next one showed a couple on their wedding day. Small white pearls adorned the bodice of the bride's dress; the man wore a black morning tuxedo, the tails elegantly curved, and pin-striped gray trousers. The woman's long hair flowed down her back, and her face glowed. She looked like a model featured in a picture frame for sale in a store. In the next photo the same couple held an infant. The infant became a young boy as I wandered down the row.

With a start, I realized it was Tommy. The young woman must be Helen. I backtracked. The shape of her eyes and her brow were the same. But that was it. I glanced over at her. Helen's chin was sharp, her shoulders poked through the thin pink cotton shirt, and the bones of her hands protruded.

"Done." Helen wiped her hands on a towel and walked over.

"I love your photos," Kelly said.

Helen nodded at the first two.

"Those are my husband's parents on their first day in this country."

I was in front of the military picture.

"That's Ken, my husband." She straightened the already neatly arranged pictures, then walked back to the kitchen and refolded a dish towel. She fussed with the vase of flowers on the dining room table, moving it a smidge to the right and then putting it back where it was.

Suddenly she covered her face with her hand for a moment, dropped it, and turned to me. She took in a deep breath. "I'm trying so hard to hold myself together. If I don't keep everything I have control over in perfect condition, I think I'll fall to pieces."

I wanted to hug her, but sometimes that was the final straw to someone's composure. She had a slim hold on her emotions right now. The neatness gave her structure.

"My husband's death, then moving here. I thought it would be a dream place for Tommy. Instead, it's become a nightmare. And then last night." She began sobbing. "Someone tried to kill my son."

"Helen, we'll find who tried to hurt Tommy. When that's behind us, we'll work on creating a life here for the two of you."

Helen wiped her eyes. "Thanks, Kelly. You have enough to do. Tommy and I will figure it out."

"No. I mean it. You haven't met Michael Corrigan yet, the owner of Resorts International. He believes employees are part of the company family, and those aren't phony corporate words. It's how he operates. We'll work this out together."

Helen went over to the table and sat.

I sat next to her and put my hand on her arm. "You'll see what I mean when you meet Michael. He'll be here Saturday."

"I'm looking forward to it." Helen straightened her back. "Where's the schedule?"

I wanted to say more, but Helen seemed to need to step back at this point. "Right here." I handed it to her. "Suzie's first at eleven. I already know what they talked about."

While Helen read the list, I looked around. Magazines were arranged in a neat stack on an end table, a newspaper folded next to them. The meticulously arranged photographs had the exact same distance between each one. Not only was nothing out of place, everything was evenly spaced.

Then chaos exploded into the room in the form of Tommy and his short-legged hound.

"Mom! Daniel said I can help him with stuff he needs to do on the van." Tommy skidded to a stop in front of her. Fred didn't have as much traction, and it took him a couple more feet on the wooden floor to come to a stop. "Is that okay?"

Daniel waved from the doorway.

"Will that work for you? He can stay here with me, you know," Helen said.

"He can be my assistant and hand me tools. He'll be a big help."

"Well, if you're sure."

"Oh boy." Tommy grabbed a bottle of juice from the fridge, and he and Fred bounded after Daniel.

Helen studied the appointment list. "I don't know what the visit to Redwood Ranch was about or who Diane is, but I know where the place is located." She pointed to the last name. "Javier is our produce supplier and a longtime friend of Bob's."

"I want to find out what Bob talked about with each of them."

"I'll jot down directions for you and bring them over." She got up, pulled open a drawer, and took out a tablet and pen.

"Sounds good." I stood. "I saw the fruit and vegetable orders when I reviewed the inn's receipts. There was contact information on them. The number for Redwood Ranch should be easy to find. I'll phone them and get my stuff."

As I walked back to the inn, I thought about what a tenuous hold Helen had on her composure. She had already been under severe stress before the attack on Tommy. The sooner the murderer was caught, the sooner she could start a new chapter in her life.

I called the sites Bob had visited and lucked out. The people on the list could see me today. I put on my fleece jacket and headed out. Helen had left the directions and the schedule on the kitchen counter while I made the calls.

I walked the short distance to Suzie's hotel. A building at the back of the inn was painted in off-white with white trim. I knocked on the door, and Suzie opened it.

"Come on in and welcome." The sparkle had returned to her voice.

I stepped into a large room with rows of wire shelves stacked to the ceiling filled with large cans and boxes. Four large steel refrigeration units lined the back wall.

"This is a nice setup. Spacious with open access to everything."

"It works really well." She held up a couple of keys. "These are what you'll need for Saturday. The shed and the refrigerators are kept locked. Transients come through town regularly, and food walks off if it's not under lock and key."

"I understand."

"The festival food will be in the first unit on the left." She pointed to a key with a red plastic cover. "This is for the refrigerator. The other one unlocks the building."

I put the keys in my fleece pocket and zipped it closed.

"What are the other two appointments? I might know something about them that would be helpful," Suzie said.

"He went to Redwood Ranch and then to Javier's produce market."

"I don't know anything about the ranch. We both had problems with the produce from Javier."

"What kinds of problems?"

"Much of it went bad shortly after delivery. Some of the strawberries already had mold on them when they arrived."

"Thanks. That'll be helpful when I talk to Javier." I checked my watch. "I'd better get going if I'm going to be back in time for us to meet at Noah's Place."

I did a fast walk back to the inn and got in the truck. I pulled out and started for Fort Paul, about fifteen minutes away. Hopefully, I'd find clues that would lead to Bob's murderer.

Chapter 23

Apainted sign over a dirt road greeted me at Redwood Ranch as I turned off Highway One. I pulled in and parked next to a dusty black pickup with several bales of alfalfa hay in the bed. I got out. A woman was tying a leopard Appaloosa to a hitching post next to a corral. His black spots ranging in size from a nickel to a silver dollar leapt out at me from his white base coat.

I walked over to her. "Hi. I'm Kelly Jackson from Redwood Cove Bed-and-Breakfast. I'm here to meet Diane."

"You found her." She finished securing the horse with a tug on the rope.

Short gray bushy hair framed her tanned face, lines deeply etched in the surface. Her denim shirt had REDWOOD RANCH embroidered in red above the pocket. She shoved a hand in my direction, and we shook.

I walked over to the horse and patted his neck. "He's a beautiful Appie."

"Sounds like you know something about horses."

"I grew up on a ranch in Wyoming. Guest ranch in the summer, working ranch year-round."

"Jackson. Are your parents Ed and Margaret?"

"Yes. How do you know them?" I was shocked at being in California and meeting a friend of my mom and dad's. Small world.

"We met at the Grand National Stock Show and Rodeo in Denver. There's an informal guest ranchers' get-together every year. We hit it off and make it a point to see each other at the event."

A young man yelled from an open barn a short distance away. "Hey, Diane, we've got a problem with one of the mares."

"I need to see what's up. I was going to give this guy some exercise in the ring. Would you like to take him for a ride?"

"Love to." I didn't realize how much I missed being on a horse until then. "What's his name?"

"Nez Perce, in honor of the Indian tribe that did a lot to develop the breed." She rubbed his forehead. "We call him Nezi for short."

The horse looked at me. I looked at him. Sizing each other up. A little rim of white showed around his eyes.

"He's a good boy," Diane said. "Jump on, and I'll adjust the stirrups."

I grabbed the saddle horn, put my foot in the stirrup, and swung my leg over. I was glad I'd chosen lightweight hiking boots as my footwear of choice for this trip. Diane quickly made the length change.

"What reining style do you use—straight or neck?"

"Neck." She opened the gate to the workout ring.

I urged Nezi forward, and Diane closed the gate.

"I'll be back in a few." She strode off.

I gave him a nudge with my legs, and we began to walk around the enclosure. He stretched out his neck, pulling extra length from the reins. I gently but firmly gathered the leather back. He shook his head. Test time. He pulled again a little harder, ears slightly back. I quickly gathered the reins in. His ears went up, and he looked back at me. Our eyes met. We had an understanding.

The rest of the workout took me back home. His gait was smooth and collected. An extra spring came through in his movement that seemed to communicate enjoyment at being in motion.

As I put him through his paces, the rhythm and paying attention to him helped calm my racing mind. Why would I want to trade doing this every day on the ranch for dealing with resort issues and, in this case, a murder? Why did I crave being able to make my own spot in the world? I'd done a good job on the ranch. It wasn't like my parents were giving me a handout.

I wasn't at peace there. That was what it was. It wasn't where I was supposed to be at this time in my life. I knew that. I'd been over it in my head so many times. I'd know when I was at the right place when I found it. I just had to trust in that.

We finished a second canter around the ring, and I slowed to a walk to cool him down. I leaned forward and patted his sweaty neck. The creak of the saddle was music to my ears.

Diane returned so I rode up to the gate, opened it, and went through. I dismounted and pulled Nezi's reins over his head. He vigorously rubbed his head against my shoulder, leaving a swath of horsehair down the arm of my fleece.

Diane grabbed the bridle and pulled him away. "Sorry about that."

"No problem. I offered a shoulder to my horse at the end of our rides. It was my way to thank her." I brushed the hair off and gave him a scratch behind the ears. "And thank you, Diane, for the ride."

"You said you wanted to talk about my meeting with Bob Phillips."

"I'm trying to find out what he was working on so I can carry on at the inn." *And maybe find out who killed him.*

"I had an idea for a riding vacation package," Diane said. "Have people stay at one inn and do different rides each day. When I asked around, Bob's name repeatedly came up as honest, easy to work with, and dependable."

There it was again. Great guy. What could have happened?

"I knew of him but hadn't had any interactions with him. He came over that day to meet me and check out my stock and the facility. I told him I wanted people to have something extra during the guests' evenings in terms of entertainment and maybe a special dinner at the inn. He was enthusiastic about it. The next step was for me to give him some dates."

"I agree it's an excellent idea. I'd like to pursue those plans with you."

"I'm glad you like it. I'll get you some dates, and we'll go from there."

I felt awkward questioning her since she didn't know Bob, but I didn't want to miss any opportunity.

"You know, Bob died later that day."

"Yeah. I read about it in the paper. Too bad." Diane studied her scuffed brown cowboy boots.

"It's hard to understand how it happened. How did he seem to you that day? Was there any indication he wasn't feeling well?"

She shrugged. "Like I said, I didn't really know him. He seemed fine to me."

Dead end there. Maybe Javier would know something.

"Give me a call, and let's go for a ride sometime. You can ride Nezi whenever he's available."

"I'd really like that." With all the thoughts swirling around in my mind, a trail ride through the countryside sounded like a perfect opportunity to clear my mind.

"It was nice meeting you. Say hi to your folks for me." She led Nezi off to the barn.

I walked slowly back to the pickup truck, breathing in the smells of the ranch. The blend of hay, animals, and the outdoors always filled me with contentment. Something I could use right now.

I glanced in the rearview mirror as I drove out. Plumes of dust billowed up behind me as I drove out to the main road, obscuring the barn and the corral. I couldn't see anything clearly. Much like my mind, glimpses of clues here and there but no clear picture.

A faded sign said PRODUCE MARKET and marked the location of Javier's store. I pulled into a parking space and got out.

Tables covered with bunches of bright green broccoli, a variety of potatoes, and other seasonal produce lined the open front of the store. I walked toward the back. A heavyset man in a canvas apron approached me.

"Can I help you?"

"I'm Kelly Jackson with Redwood Cove Bed-and-Breakfast. I called earlier and spoke with Javier."

"That's me. You wanted to know about my appointment with Bob."

"I'm trying to get up to speed on what the issues are at the inn. I understand you supply all the fruit and vegetables."

"Right. Recently some of it wasn't the quality Bob expected. He brought me some samples. I checked into it and found out one of my new drivers hadn't taken the necessary precautions during a hot spell. That's taken care of now."

"I reviewed the invoices from past orders. It seems like what's needed is pretty routine."

"It is. Bob and I talked on the phone about what was in season, and he'd make his order. Sometimes he came by and did it in person. When he did, we always got together for coffee. We've been friends for fifteen years." He stopped and looked down. "We were friends for fifteen years."

"I'm sorry. I know it's been a shock for everyone."

"I wish we'd sat down together that day. Maybe he'd still be alive." His voice trembled, and he turned away to arrange some already neatly stacked apples.

"What happened that you didn't follow the usual routine?" Okay, that could come across as being nosy, but what people thought of me right now didn't matter.

Javier kept arranging apples. "We'd planned on it. He stepped outside to answer a call on his cell phone. I heard his raised voice." He turned back to me. "Very unusual for Bob to do that. When he came back in, I could tell he was upset. I asked if everything was all right. He said it was just something he had to deal with and he'd have to pass on coffee. He had to meet someone."

That someone was probably the last person to see Bob alive according to my timeline. The murderer.

"Do you have any idea who he was meeting?"

"Nope."

"Do you know if it was business or personal? It might be something I need to follow up on."

"Not a clue."

"What time did he leave?"

"I think it was around two thirty."

I thanked Javier for the information and made an order for the inn. I started up the truck and began the drive back. No wonder the killer had wanted that cell phone. It would show who had called him. I agreed with Stanton that it was long gone, but not for the money it could bring in. It was probably at the bottom of the ocean by now. We could get the phone records, but it would take a while.

What had I found out? Bob met with Suzie about the festival and arranged to pick up the keys for the refrigerator and the shed. Nothing there. Same with the information from the ranch. I decided to drive out to where Bob was found to find out how long it took to get there. The clock on the dashboard displayed one ten. Twenty minutes later I parked where Daniel had stopped the other day. Bob's body was found at three thirty. The person who found him said he didn't see anyone else. Bob left the market at two thirty. With the drive and the walk to where he was found, that would make it about three. An argument, a shove, and the murderer had time to disappear.

The person he talked to on the phone had to be the killer.

Chapter 24

Thirty minutes later I was on my way to meet Suzie. As I turned the corner to head for Noah's Place, I caught sight of her gleaming yellow curls a half a block ahead of me.

"Suzie. Wait up!"

The young woman turned and waved. I picked up my pace.

"I appreciate your help with this." I fell in step with her.

"Kelly, anybody who would do what they did to Tommy deserves to be caught and punished." Suzie's mouth was set in a grim line, an uncharacteristic expression for her.

"I'd like you to ask the questions. I'll chime in if I think of something."

"Got it." Suzie opened the door to the café.

Noah was in the back of the kitchen.

Suzie peered in. "Hey, Noah. Is this a good time to talk?"

He nodded but kept his focus on the large ball of dough he was kneading. "I can work and talk, too. No problem."

"You probably heard about what happened at the headlands last night," Suzie said.

"Yep. The town's buzzing." He whacked the dough with the palm of his hand. A deep frown creased his forehead.

"We're trying to help find out who attacked Tommy."

Noah looked at us. "I keep thinking about my son and how I'd feel if someone tried to hurt him." He pounded the dough into the wooden block. "The rage I'd feel." He flattened the dough with a series of punches.

"We thought if you could tell us who was here at seven thirty last night, which is when it happened, that would rule them out, narrow the field of suspects," Suzie said.

"Do you think it was a local?" His gaze never left the dough.

"We have no idea. We want to make a list of who couldn't have been involved."

"The band took a break about then, and people ordered. The place was packed. I can picture a lot of their faces. George Johnson, Fred McCrae, Gordon Jones, to name a few. I can write names down for you this afternoon." He grabbed a towel from a nearby rack and wiped the flour from his hands.

"That would be great. What time should I come by to get it?"

"I'll have it ready for you by four."

I fingered the paper menu on the counter. "We're concerned the person might try again. Is there anyone you know who left right after I did? We could start there for now. Try to find out what they were doing last night."

Noah went back to kneading the dough, not answering right away. Seconds passed.

Had I overstepped my bounds? Had the invisible door slammed shut on the outsider?

He stopped working and stared at me. "I served Tommy ice cream night before last. I'm glad he's okay, and I'm glad I'll be able to hand him another ice cream cone."

I almost shivered from the cold shoulder I felt Noah was giving me.

But then he said, "Andy and Phil left right after you. They had festival work to do, they said."

Yikes. Two of the four.

"Suzie, your employee, Jason, took off. Said he really wanted to stay but had to do prep for tomorrow."

"He did. Jason's handling the booth for our hotel."

Number three.

"Charlie Chan got a call and canceled a food order he'd just placed. Said there was an emergency."

And number four.

Suzie and Noah talked about a couple of other people who'd left . . . a dad needing to babysit, a plumber with a leaky pipe to fix.

I had tuned out. All four possible suspects had left in time to attack Tommy. Did any of them have alibis? And how was I going to find out?

Chapter 25

"What's your next step?" Suzie asked as we walked out of Noah's Place.

"Clear the four men who left right after I did." If that was possible.

"How are you going to do that?"

"Find out where they were when Tommy was attacked."

"You're really getting into this."

"I need to take some action. I refuse to wait until something else happens."

"I can help. I left a few minutes after you did. I saw Jason when I stopped by the hotel's restaurant on my way home. He was preparing desserts for the festival."

"Good. That's one off the list."

"I hope the others get cleared, as well." Suzie's voice held a worried note.

"I do, too." Boy, did I ever. Two of them were staying at the inn, and Charlie came by on a regular basis. They all had way too much access to Tommy.

We got to the corner. "Thanks for helping. I don't think Noah would've been willing to talk to me the way he did, without you there."

"Glad to do it." Suzie placed her hand on my arm. "I hope you find who is at the bottom of this . . . but be careful."

I was moved by the concern in Suzie's eyes. "I will."

"I'll pick up the list from Noah this afternoon and drop it at the inn," Suzie said.

"I appreciate it. We have a lot of arrivals today." Including one I had mixed feelings about. Scott. When would he arrive?

"Call if you need anything else." With a wave and a smile, Suzie was off.

Wrapping the dark blue company fleece jacket tightly around me, I picked up my pace. A gray cloud of fog lingered off the coast. Khaki-clad tourists with shopping bags resting at their feet had replaced the early morning locals at the coffeehouse.

I entered the inn and appreciated the warmth of the kitchen after the cold ocean breeze. Phil and Andy sat next to each other in the workroom with several folders in front of them.

"Hi, guys. Festival planning?"

"Yep. We have a meeting in the conference room in"—Andy glanced at his watch—"twenty minutes."

I put my fanny pack on the counter. How could I find out what Andy and Phil had done last night? I could just ask, but that seemed pretty intrusive. I didn't know them well. They weren't aware I knew they left right after me. Maybe if I assumed they were there, they'd tell me where they'd gone.

"Phil, I really enjoyed your dance last night. Did you do any more?"

"No. We decided it was time for dessert and left shortly after that." He patted the files. "And we needed to work."

"Where did you go? Is it a place we could recommend to guests?" I forced casualness into my voice.

"We came back here and felt there was every reason to mix business and pleasure." He appeared pleased with himself. "Which we did. I supplied a fabulous dessert wine. A ten-year-old tawny port."

Andy stood, bowed, and gave a grandiose wave of his arm in the direction of the refrigerator. "And I provided Etorki, a pasteurized sheep's milk cheese made in the French Basque region of the Pyrenees. A hint of caramel in its creamy texture, a buttery aroma—a delight for the senses!" He put his fingers together and did an air-kiss to the tips of his fingers—the universal gesture for magnificent.

He headed to the fridge. "There's some left. Would you like to try it?" He was like a child ready to get into a box of candy as he pulled out a plastic-wrapped tray. His eyes widened as he began to uncover the cheese.

"Thanks, Andy," I said quickly. "I'd love to, but another time. It seems all I've been doing is eating since I got here."

Andy gazed longingly at the plate. He slowly replaced it on the refrigerator shelf.

Phil laughed. "Andy, there'll be final details to wrap up for tomorrow. We can enjoy your cheese then."

Andy perked up and closed the refrigerator door.

I hadn't seen them when I got back from Noah's Place. Where had they been working? Again, asking outright seemed pretty nosy. I thought for a few minutes as I grabbed a cup and poured some coffee. The aroma of the strong Italian roast pushed my brain into gear.

"Did you see or hear anything when you returned? We're trying to get as much information as we can because of what happened to Tommy."

The smile disappeared from Andy's face. "No. My room has a fairly large desk and an alcove. We decided to discuss the festival up there so we wouldn't be interrupted."

"Thanks. I'll let you get back to work. Please let me know if you remember anything else." I headed for my room.

Andy and Phil provided alibis for each other. There were two people involved in the attack on Tommy. As much as I liked them, I still couldn't rule them out.

Charlie Chan. How was I going to find out about him? I doubted he was due back here for a while. Driving around town trying to spot him didn't seem like the smartest move. He could be in Fort Paul for all I knew.

What would bring him back here? Needing more water. But there was plenty. A failed water cooler? How could I make that happen? I stopped at the door to my room, turned, and headed back to the kitchen.

Excited chatter came from the conference room as I passed. It sounded like the meeting was underway.

The cooler resided in a corner of the workroom near the computer station. White plastic knobs were recessed into the back of the unit. No easy accidental breakage could occur by something hitting them. I flicked one up and down. I could forcibly break it, but how would I explain that?

I stepped back and surveyed the room. There were a couple of other places the water container would fit. New manager decides to rearrange furniture, cooler gets knocked over. That could work. I wanted to damage it just enough to require a visit.

But wait. I wanted to see Charlie, and he delivered water. They might send someone else for a repair. What I needed was a reason to have more water delivered. The sound of boisterous voices floated down the hall.

The festival! That was the answer.

The number for the water company was posted above the phone. "Hello, this is Kelly Jackson at Redwood Cove Bed-and-Breakfast. There's going to be an event on our grounds tomorrow, and I'd like to have additional water. Would it be possible to have some delivered today? I know it's late to make a request like this."

"Let me put you on hold while I contact the driver," said the company rep.

I crossed my fingers and willed the answer to be the one I wanted.

"Good news. Our truck hasn't made the Redwood Cove drops yet, and he has extra bottles on board. How many would you like?"

I grabbed a number. "Three."

"No problem. They'll be there this afternoon."

"Thanks." I hung up. Luck was with me. Now if only Charlie delivered the water.

The phone rang as I started to turn away, and I picked it up. "Redwood Cove Bed-and-Breakfast. Kelly speaking." I was surprised at how automatic the answer had become.

"Hi, Kelly, how are you doing?"

I knew the voice went with a James Bond look-alike—one of the tall, dark-haired, attractive ones.

"Scott, how nice to hear your voice." Was it? I wanted to handle the inn on my own, and I didn't want emotional complications in my life.

"I wanted to let you know I'm in Cloverdale. I'll probably be there in about an hour and a half."

"Oh good." Sounding enthusiastic was a struggle.

"Kelly, I know this is your first solo job." He paused. "I remember my first one and how important it was to me. I'm only coming because it's company policy when police have been involved in serious incidents at one of our sites."

I sighed. "I know. Michael explained that to me when I was hired."

"I'll stay in the background. I can help out at the festival." Another pause. "I'll just be there."

I was touched but not surprised. Kind. Sensitive. Smart. Those attributes went on the Scott list, as well. Mr. Perfect. "Thanks for understanding, Scott."

"Great, then. See you soon."

"'Bye." At least this complication wasn't life-threatening. Or was it, in a different way? It had felt like my life was over when I found out my husband had been cheating on me. I didn't feel ready to risk being hurt again.

What could I do next? I wondered if the game warden had found out anything. Had the Sentinels decoded the last page of notes?

As if on cue, there was a knock at the back door. Its window framed the Professor's face. I waved him in.

"Hi, Professor. What brings you here?"

"We deciphered another page of notes." He pulled a piece of paper from his pocket. "I thought you might like a copy before I deliver it to Fran." He handed the paper to me.

"You must have been reading my mind. I wondered if you'd learned anything more." I scanned the page. "Is there anything that stands out?"

"Not really. The number of abalone taken increased." He sat on a nearby stool and placed his plaid wool cap on the counter. "Whoever's poaching is making a lot of money." He fingered the hat's soft cloth—a blend of subtle red, green, and gray threads. "Hundreds of thousands of dollars."

"I know you believe Bob was murdered. Do you think this is why?"

"Good possibility. He wanted so much to help, to save our land and resources for future generations and for his grandkids." Sadness weighed down his voice. His shoulders drooped. "I think Bob got in over his head."

"Do you have any idea who might have killed him?"

He looked at me. "Yes."

Chapter 26

My heart raced. Maybe we could finally put an end to this craziness.

The Professor leaned forward and whispered in a conspiratorial manner. "It has to be someone with connections in the Bay Area and who travels there a lot." He sat back and winked at me knowingly.

My soaring hopes crash-landed with a jolt. "I'd been thinking along the same lines, Professor." I struggled to keep the disappointment off my face.

"The amount of abalone they're taking means it has to be shuttled out of here often." He pulled another piece of paper from his pocket and handed it to me. "Here's who I came up with so far."

I examined the list. My four top suspects were there plus three others. If the stolen BlackBerry was connected, the new people weren't in the running.

I lowered my voice. "I'm checking on Andy, Phil, Jason, and Charlie."

He patted my hand. "I know it must be hard. They seem to be really nice men, but we have to consider everyone."

"I agree, Professor."

"I didn't know you were investigating them. The Silver Sentinels will work on the other three."

"I don't know if *investigating* is the right word. I've been gathering information."

"Nonsense, my dear. You're tracking down a murderer."

Tracking down a murderer. Somehow I hadn't thought of it in those terms before. I was finding out what happened to Bob and Tommy . . . I was tracking down a murderer. I swallowed hard.

"The Silver Sentinels had a meeting yesterday. Maybe you felt your ears burning." He smiled. "We appreciate the help and support you've given us. You're too young to become a member of the Silver Sentinels, but we've decided to offer you an associate membership." The Professor tilted his head. "Will you join us, my dear?"

I hesitated. "Professor, I don't know how long I'll be here."

"That's no problem. Besides, with Internet communication, the world is becoming one large community."

"I have one caveat. My obligations to Resorts International come first."

"Of course. This is your career. You have a loyalty to your employer."

"Then I'd love to join your group, and I'm honored."

"Superb. I'll let the others know."

Crunching gravel outside announced the arrival of a vehicle. I glanced out the back window. A green sedan with a FISH AND GAME logo on its side rolled to a stop. The door opened, and Fran Cartwright thrust out a sturdy, uniform-clad leg. Her close-cropped silver hair glinted in the sun.

"Ahh, the renderer of justice arrives." The Professor tapped the list with a long, slender finger. "Why don't you make a copy of this for yourself?"

"Good idea. I'm not familiar with the three other people."

"Would you please make two copies of the deciphered notes? You can have one, and Fran can have the other."

"You bet." I walked over to the copier as the Professor opened the back door for the warden.

"Hey, everyone. How's it going?" Fran stepped into the room.

"Hello, Fran," the Professor responded. "Thanks for coming."

"Are you kidding? I got here as fast as I could when I heard you had more information."

I folded my two pages and tucked them into one of my jeans pockets. I handed the Professor his originals and Fran her copy of the deciphered notes.

Noises from the hallway heralded the end of the festival meeting. Andy and Phil entered the room with Jason close behind.

A stout man passed by saying, "In the morning I'm heading for the double chocolate truffles first thing." He rubbed his hands together. "They sound so fantastic."

"Great. We won't be competing," said his lanky friend. "I want the first taste of the cabernet ice cream with chocolate drizzles."

They laughed.

"Tomorrow's going to be a treat, as always," said the heavier man.

Several other people I didn't recognize filed through and out, everyone grinning and commenting on how they were looking forward to tomorrow.

The water delivery van pulled in and parked as members of the group descended the steps. Charlie Chan got out and opened the truck's side door.

Thank goodness. Charlie was making the delivery. But how was I going to question him with all the ruckus around me?

Charlie strode up the steps and walked through the open door, where people were still exiting.

"I'll just take this and go." Fran held up the paper. "The abalone poachers I arrested are close to cutting a deal. I'm hoping this information will be the final straw."

"Marvelous news, Warden," the Professor said. "I'm glad the Silver Sentinels could help."

"Later, guys." Fran made her exit.

The Professor turned to me. "Time for me to depart, as well. I'll be in touch." He started to leave, then stopped. "This may sound like a bit of an odd request, but do you mind if I watch the construction of the tent for tomorrow? I've always been fascinated by how fast they can create a huge, temporary building."

He struck me as someone with an always-inquiring mind. "Certainly. Stay as long as you like."

Charlie shifted from side to side and slapped his clipboard against his palm.

Andy walked to the refrigerator, opened it, and pulled the cheese platter out. He inclined his head toward the hallway to Jason and Phil. "Let's go to my room and finish our plans there. I've got crackers and Pellegrino to go with this."

"Pellegrino?" Phil questioned. "But that's water. What kind of a Greek drinks water with fine cheese?"

"You're certainly welcome to provide a beverage of your choice," Andy replied.

"I'll stop by my room for a bottle of 2006 Nelsen merlot and glasses," Phil said.

The three headed down the hall, discussions of the chocolate and wine festival drifting in my direction.

Now it was just Charlie and me. Question time. I decided to do what I did with Phil and Andy and assume he'd stayed at Noah's Place.

"Hi, Kelly. I heard you wanted some extra water?" He looked quizzically at the porch where seven bottles were lined up.

"Y . . . yes." I stuttered a bit. "I . . . I don't know how many people will be at the festival, but I want to be sure to have enough." Sounded lame to me, but it was the best I could do on short notice.

He shrugged. "Sure. Whatever. Better safe than sorry, as they say." He walked out to his truck, with me tagging along.

"I enjoyed Phil's dance last night. Did he do more after I left?"

"Don't know. Friend called. Had to leave." He heaved a bottle onto his hand truck and began bumping it up the stairs.

I followed. "Nothing serious, I hope."

"Nope."

So . . . now what? Sleuthing isn't looking like a promising career at the moment.

I trailed him back down to the truck, beginning to feel like a stray dog begging for crumbs. "I'm glad to hear that." Dead in the water. I'd irritated him before with my questions. I gazed off at the ocean as he put the remaining two bottles on the deck, racking my brain for some question I could ask to find out more.

A member of the cavalry saved me. The horse was a white Chevrolet with Deputy Sheriff Stanton at the reins. He pulled in next to Charlie's delivery truck.

The officer shuffled a few papers on the seat of his car and then pushed the door open.

"Charlie, Kelly, good to see you." He got out. "Charlie, I need to ask you some questions about last night. I called your company, and they told me your route."

Great! Maybe I can learn something.

Charlie put his hand truck back in the van. "E-mail and cell phones have been sizzling. It's about what happened to the kid, right?"

The deputy nodded. "Yep. Talking to as many people as possible. With the work you do, you cover a lot of territory."

"I don't know of anything that might help you, but I'm happy to talk."

"The office is still available," I said to the deputy.

Deputy Sheriff Stanton turned to me. "Thanks for the offer. I'll take you up on it."

"Would either of you like coffee?"

Both responded with an affirmative nod.

We walked back into the kitchen, and I started a fresh pot of coffee. There was some already there, but I wanted an excuse to get into the study during the questioning.

"It won't take long to brew. I'll bring it to you as soon as it's finished."

"Thanks, Ms. Jackson," Stanton said.

The two men walked to the office.

And when I deliver the coffee, maybe I'll hear something helpful.

I pulled down two mugs and then reviewed the guest list. Only a few people left to go for checking in.

The coffeepot finally uttered its last spluttering noises. I filled the cups, put them on a tray along with cream and sugar, and went down the hallway. I paused a minute at the door to see if I could hear anything. I told myself that eavesdropping was permitted when there was a murder and an attempted murder to solve.

Nothing. The oak door was thick and solid. I knocked.

"Come on in." Deputy Stanton had moved the chair behind the desk around so he could face Charlie. Stanton was leaning toward him, hands clasped. He glanced up as I came in.

"Could be." Charlie nodded his head.

I placed the tray on the desk. "Here you go." I handed them their coffee.

"Thanks. Last night was a long night," the deputy said.

Charlie nodded. "End of my shift, and I'm dragging. This'll definitely help."

Both men looked at me expectantly . . . and they weren't talking.

Talk to each other. I'm just the waitress, the maid. Ignore me.

"Can I get you anything else?" I almost felt like curtsying, but I didn't think it would quite work with my jeans.

"No thanks," Deputy Stanton said.

Charlie affirmed the deputy's response with a negative shake of his head.

They waited patiently. The silence lengthened. It was clear my departure was what they wanted.

"See you then." I left. No luck there.

I went to my room to pack for the night. It wouldn't take long. I'd only been here two days and I'd been on the go most of the time. I traveled light. Not much time to get ready when the phone call came in from the boss.

I called Esther, head of housekeeping, and told her my plans. She said she'd send someone over to prepare my room for Helen and Tommy.

Suddenly, the quiet afternoon exploded with noise.

"Stop! No move," someone roared.

Only one person I knew had that kind of volume.

"Miss Kelly! Miss Kelly!" Ivan bellowed.

The sound came from the kitchen. I ran.

Ivan's eyebrows arched so high they blended with his hairline. His face was an ominous red.

Scott sat at the counter, blue eyes shining, an amused smile on his face. His usual uniform of neatly pressed tan slacks, navy blazer, and white shirt fit him well.

"Kelly, it's good to see you." He slid off the stool and gave me a quick hug. "It's been a while."

"He boyfriend?" Ivan's face turned from red to purple.

"No!" I almost shouted.

"He hug. He boyfriend."

Scott raised an eyebrow, and his smile grew wider. I could see he was enjoying this way too much. He looked at me hopefully. "Boyfriend?"

I glared at him.

The commotion drew others to the room. Daniel came in as Ivan declared my relationship to Scott. Allie trailed behind him.

Daniel appeared surprised but held his hand out to Scott. "Daniel Stevens. Glad to meet you." They shook. "This is my daughter, Allie." He put his arm around her shoulders.

"Boyfriend! Cool," Allie declared with an expression only a teenage girl could get when boyfriends were discussed.

Helen, Tommy, and Fred had followed them in.

"Kelly's boyfriend. How nice you could come for a visit," Helen said.

"Wait!" I tried to stop the stampede of words around me, but it didn't happen.

"I'm Tommy, and this is Fred." The boy pointed to the tricolored dog bouncing up and down at his side, excited by all the commotion.

"Hold it, folks." I held up my hands, finally reining in the runaway conversation. "Let's get things straight. This is Scott Thompson. He's an administrator with Resorts International. Not a boyfriend. A work associate."

I explained the company policy as Ivan's face regained its normal color.

"Sorry. I see walk in back door, no knock," Ivan rumbled in his best attempt at a quiet voice.

"I apologize for the upset. I've been here numerous times before," Scott said. "I knew Bob and his wife and always stopped by to chat when I was in the area. I often stayed in the visiting manager's room."

Ivan shuffled his feet. "I watch for strangers. Protecting boy."

It hit me, and I felt like I'd been thrown from a horse and landed on packed dirt. "You've been taking shifts. Rudy, Mary, and the Professor." I'd been slow on this one. The Silver Sentinels had been watching over Tommy.

"We want to help," the bear-sized member of the Sentinels announced. "Gertie here earlier."

Helen went over and gave Ivan a hug, or at least the best she could do considering his size. It was more of a front body clasp. Tears began to trickle down her cheeks.

"Thank you. I had no idea people cared so much."

"We are the Silver Sentinels. We care. We protect." He patted her awkwardly on the back. Then his chest puffed up. The bravado that had slipped away during the boyfriend confusion flowed back. "We care. We protect."

"Right, then," Scott said. "Now that we've gotten that straightened out, where should I put my things?"

Oh my gosh. My deer-in-the-headlights look tipped Scott to the situation.

"Okay. I'm guessing there *is* nowhere for me to put my things."

"I'm . . . I'm so sorry. It . . . it all happened so fast. Your coming here, I mean. And besides, there hasn't been room for weeks because of the festival. And . . ."

"Kelly, no problem," Scott said. "We'll figure something out."

"But how? The company policy says we both need to be on site."

"He can have my room," Tommy piped up.

The room silenced. No one said a word.

Right. House a top executive administrator in a little boy's room. The proverbial pin could drop, and we'd all hear it.

"And where do you live, Tommy?" Scott knelt down and scratched Fred's ears.

"I live in the little house over there." He pointed at the cottage visible through the back door window.

"That's very generous of you. Where will you stay?"

"Miss Kelly wants my mom and me to stay in her room tonight." He faltered a bit. "Because of what happened to me." Tommy sat on the floor and put his arms around Fred's neck and held him close.

Scott looked at me. "And where are you staying, Miss Kelly?"

"In Helen's room." I paused for a moment. "In the cottage."

"Perfect, then." Scott straightened up. "You and I will share a small bed-and-breakfast."

Two bedrooms.

One shared bathroom.

Small.

Very small.

Chapter 27

My throat was suddenly tight. "That should work."

Helen glanced at the clock. "There's enough time before I put out the beverages and hors d'oeuvres for me to change sheets and put out towels for you two."

"I'll take care of the food," I said.

"Are you sure? That's part of my job."

"You have plenty to do with packing for the night."

"Thanks. That's sweet of you. Everything is prepared, waiting in the refrigerator, and ready to go."

"C'mon, Mr. Scott," Tommy said, "I'll show you my room. You can even play with my Legos if you want. But please don't take apart the ones on my bookshelf."

"That's very nice of you, Tommy." Scott gave me a wink. "Let's go."

Tall man, short boy, and trotting dog left for the cottage. Helen and Allie followed closely behind.

"I go now. Enough people here," Ivan said.

"Ivan, please thank the Silver Sentinels for their vigilance." I looked at him with affection. "It's greatly appreciated by all of us, and I'm going to let my boss know how much your group has done."

"You welcome." He placed his black wool fisherman's cap on his head and gave it a strong tug on the brim, securing it against the ever-present coastal winds.

Daniel flipped through the notes he'd taken at the cottage. "I'm going to order pizza tonight for Helen, Tommy, Allie, and myself. We'll eat at their place. That way I can stay with them while they're getting their things together."

"Thanks for all of your help." I sighed. "I hope they catch the person soon."

"Me, too." Daniel filed his papers in a plastic tray on the wall. "Would you like me to order a pizza for you and Scott?"

"No thanks. I appreciate the offer, but I've been enjoying way too many wonderful things not listed on my usual low cal diet."

"I'll walk Helen and Tommy over about eight."

"Sounds like a plan."

Daniel left to join the others.

I spied a tray with two empty cups on the counter. That explained why Stanton and Charlie hadn't joined the ruckus. Had the deputy learned anything helpful? I doubted he'd tell me if he had. Was there any way I could get Charlie to tell me about their discussion? Unlikely, but I'd try to find him tomorrow and give it a shot.

I went back to my room to finish packing.

Scott. What an awkward situation. While I struggled to keep him at a distance, Fate kept throwing us together. Should I be paying attention to the murmurs of the Universe?

I shook my head. No, not now. Someone had tried to kill Tommy, and I believed Bob was murdered. Finding out who was responsible was where my focus needed to be.

Sitting down on the window seat, I pulled out the two pieces of paper and unfolded them. Putting the list of suspects down on the couch, I studied the deciphered notes. They were similar to the ones I'd already seen. The Navajo words *BESH-LAGAI* and *CH-CHIL-BE* had silver and gold written next to them followed by *3P*. Spidery handwriting under them read: *money? color? Three PM*. It would seem likely it had to do with money because of how much the abalone poachers were raking in. Maybe the time was when the money changed hands. But why two words? Was it something to do with how the payment was made? If they were colors, what did they refer to? Someone's clothes? Jewelry? Color of cars? I could check on the vehicles tomorrow.

I shook my head. Enough for now. Time to get ready. My light blue fleece hung from the back of the wooden chair at the table. I grabbed it and put it on top of my duffel bag. I reached under the pillow, pulled out my pajamas, and paused. They were my favorite ones—navy blue with running, cream-colored horses. Perfect for the ranch but probably not executive administrator wear. While I didn't intend to parade around for anyone in my nightclothes, things could happen. I found a terry-cloth robe in the closet and tried it on. It stopped at my knees. Still lots of equines showing. Better than nothing. I threw it on top of the bag.

The bell rang, announcing the arrival of a guest. After I checked in a young couple from Berkeley, I walked back to my room, got my things, and carried them to the kitchen. I could see Scott walking toward the inn with a large bundle in his arms. I put my bags in a corner and opened the door.

"Thanks," he said.

Now I could see he was carrying a large, forest-green dog bed.

"My new job—Fred's butler." He held up the bed. "Where should I put it, madam?" he asked with a prim and proper English accent.

"My room's open. You can put it anywhere in there."

He walked by, and I did a double take. He wore faded jeans, a tan flannel shirt, and lightweight hiking boots. That wasn't what he'd worn when we worked together in Colorado. Where was the perfectly attired business executive?

I started pulling out plates for the evening treats, wondering about this new side of Scott.

He returned, announcing, "Mission accomplished. I hope my new boss won't be too demanding." He grinned. "Baked dog treats? Heated kibble?"

I smiled. "Fred's pretty easygoing. I don't think you need to worry." I glanced at him as I arranged the plates on trays. "When we worked together at Keane Manor, you only wore ironed khakis, pressed crease down the front, starched white shirts, and loafers. I didn't know you even owned blue jeans."

"When Michael called about the situation in Colorado, I was on my way back from an extensive series of business meetings. I had casual wear, but it wasn't a jeans-type trip. I only had time to change flights and fly straight to the resort."

Bemused, I sat at the counter and leaned back into its rounded edge.

"So, yes, Ms. Jackson, I wear jeans. I even have denim shirts, work boots, T-shirts with logos on them, old tennis shoes, caps from various events, sweats . . ."

"Okay, okay." I laughed. "I get it."

"Three days in Colorado dealing with the situation we had isn't exactly the best way to get to know someone," Scott said.

"Agreed."

"Speaking of which, I'd like to hear about what's been happening here and learn more about the Silver Sentinels." He grabbed a loaner jacket from a peg by the door. "I can go to Shadelands Market and get a roasted chicken. They also have prepared salads and side dishes. I'll put something together for us. We can talk over dinner."

"Great idea." This was a different Scott than the one I had met previously. Casual. Easygoing. Relaxed. And in jeans, no less.

The doorbell rang as Scott left. The final guests for the weekend had arrived. After checking them in, I went back to the kitchen and finished assembling the wine and appetizers. As I took them to the parlor, the suspects paraded through my mind yet again. Could I get Stanton to tell me anything? I picked up the bottles of wine from the counter that had been opened and took them to the parlor. What excuse did I have for calling him?

Bingo!

The Professor's list and their investigation. I had more information for him. I could also tell him about their watching over Tommy.

Perfect.

I punched in Stanton's cell number, memorized by now.

"Deputy Sheriff Stanton."

"Hi, it's Kelly Jackson."

"Hello, Ms. Jackson. What can I do for you?"

Did I catch a hint of reserve? Maybe wondering what I was bringing his way this time?

"I thought you might like to know what the Silver Sentinels have been up to, and I have more news for you."

"Right. What are my active seniors into now?"

I explained about the Professor's plans and the watch group.

"Sounds like something they'd do. And I agree with the Professor. We've been pursuing the same line."

"Were you able to find out anything from Charlie?" I forced a light, happy voice that was becoming all too familiar.

His sigh traveled clearly over the phone. "Ms. Jackson, you know I can't talk to you about that."

Rats. "Can you tell me if he has an alibi?"

There was a long moment of silence. "If what he told me checks out, he has an alibi."

"Thanks for the information. Do you know what kind of vehicle he drives?"

"A small Chevrolet pickup with a white camper shell. Why?"

"It goes back to the Professor's and my theory the abalone poachers have to work with someone who has connections in San Francisco. Charlie's family is there, and he visits regularly. They also have to have a vehicle that could transport the bags of abalone."

"Good thinking, Ms. Jackson," the deputy sheriff said.

"What color is his vehicle?" No reason to miss an opportunity to gain as much information as possible.

"Silver. Why do you ask?"

"The latest page of notes the Sentinels deciphered has the words *silver* and *gold*. It probably refers to money, but someone jotted down color with a question mark. I'm keeping an open mind."

"Again, good thinking. What else was in the notes?"

I filled him in. "Do you know what the others on our list drive?"

"Andy's got a gold van, and Jason's is white. I'm not sure about Phil."

"Thanks for the information. I can find out what Phil drives."

"Anything else?"

"That's it. I hope you don't have any unpleasant surprises this evening."

"Me, too." He hung up.

Silver and gold. Interesting. My car list was well underway. If the colors were connected to vehicles, that would eliminate Jason.

I felt good about providing some information that might prove useful to the investigation. I hummed as I finished putting out the evening's offerings, started a fire, and began to set the counter for Scott and me. I pulled silverware and napkins from the drawer and dishes from the cupboard. My mind kept churning. Charlie had a vehicle that would work for delivering abalone. Deputy Sheriff Stanton hadn't yet checked the alibi. Charlie was still in the running.

Scott opened the door as I was putting out wineglasses. He put a large paper bag down on the counter, and we worked together to unload the contents. The chicken was a perfect shade of brown and smelled divine. He'd put together a large green salad with a myriad of additions. I could see small yellow and red tomatoes, green onions, and black beans, among other things. Several small containers of salad dressing appeared. A box of herbed potatoes rounded out the dinner. I liked his choices.

I pulled a bottle of Rose Winery 2006 chardonnay from the refrigerator, took out the cork, and poured some for us.

We both sat with a mutual sigh.

"It's good to see you again." He held up his wine, and we clinked our glasses together. "Please catch me up to speed with what's been happening."

We ate, talked, and took occasional trips to the parlor to check on provisions and the fire for the guests. By the time we finished dinner, he knew what I knew. By the time we'd cleared dishes together, he knew what I suspected.

"What are your next steps, Kelly?"

Before I could answer, Tommy, Helen, and Fred came in. Daniel and Allie waved from the door and said their good-byes.

"My room's open. Here are the keys." I handed them to Helen. "Everyone's checked in. The fire is dying down. However, there are still a few trays to pick up."

"I'll take care of them. Tommy can help me." Helen's eyes looked larger than usual due to the dark circles under them. "Thanks again, Kelly."

"Happy to help."

"Time to be off to our B&B." Scott grinned at me.

Inwardly I groaned. Outwardly I smiled, picked up my bags, and grabbed a flashlight from the ones by the door. *Here we go.*

We let ourselves out the back and heard Helen slide the dead bolt home.

I turned on the flashlight and lit the path to the cottage a short distance away.

The lights were on when we entered. I had only been in the home once. It had been clear Helen was a meticulous housekeeper, and that hadn't changed. We walked down the short hallway off of the living room. Helen's room was on the left. A dark oak double bed with matching bureau furnished the room along with a vanity table and chair. I put my bags down.

Tommy's room was on the other side. I looked in. A plethora of stuffed animals, books, and models filled every corner and shelf. The bed had a pile of fluffy dogs on it, with one bearing a resemblance to Fred at the front of the heap. The Legos occupied a special area all to themselves on a large bookcase.

Posters of all kinds of dogs papered the wall. German shepherds, bloodhounds, Chihuahuas, and poodles were among the many. While dogs were clearly his favorite, the ceiling had images of soaring eagles, majestic white cranes, and a pair of quail with a passel of fluff balls following them. The bedspread rained cats and dogs. Animal eyes peered from every nook and cranny.

"Are you sure about this? We could fix the couch for you."

"What? And miss this opportunity to regain my childhood by sleeping in the lad's room?"

"Thanks for being such a good sport."

"No problem." He gestured to the tiny bathroom separating the two rooms. "Ladies first to the facilities. I'm going to read for a bit."

We said our good nights. After I brushed my teeth, I changed into my flannel pajamas and folded the floral-patterned bedspread down to the foot of the bed. Nestling under the down comforter was heaven.

Darn. I forgot to floss. I eyed my clothes and the robe. Which should I put on? The robe covered most of my ranch pajamas. I hadn't heard any noise from Scott for a while. It would be a quick trip to the bathroom. I wanted to get back to the warm bed as soon as possible.

I put on the robe, picked up the flashlight, and opened the door an inch. There was a light under Tommy's door, but I didn't hear any movement. Tiptoeing to the bathroom caused only a few creaks from the aged wooden floor. I closed the bathroom door, flossed, and got ready to dash back to my room. I opened the door and peeked out. All clear. I took a step, and Scott came out of Tommy's room.

Caught. Murphy's Law at work.

He grinned. "Time to brush my teeth and call it a day." He glanced downward, and the grin widened. "You have animals running all over your clothes."

"Yes, I know." I lifted my chin as the raging heat of a blush engulfed my face and silently dared him to say another word.

He opened his mouth, closed it, and said, " 'Night, then." He turned to the bathroom. "I hope the sound of galloping hooves doesn't keep you awake tonight."

I closed the bedroom door a little harder than necessary. If running horses kept me up, I hoped a few of those Legos would come alive and clomp around his room.

Chapter 28

The alarm buzzed, and I reached over and pushed down the button. Snuggling into the cloudlike covering of down, I relished the warmth. But only for a moment. It was hard to get up, but sleeping in was a luxury that would have to wait. I threw the covers back and turned on the lamp next to the bed. The soft glow revealed the oak nightstand. Its sheen spoke of years of polishing. I rolled out of bed and put on the workout suit I'd placed on a chair last night. I preferred morning for exercising. It was so much easier when I was still half-asleep.

I flipped the switch for the overhead lights and began the series of kicks and punches I had put together. A chair went flying and hit the wall, the accidental recipient of a back kick. I bent down and straightened it.

"Kelly, are you okay?" Scott shouted and pounded on the door.

"I'm fine." I rushed to the mirror over the bureau. My bangs stood straight up. I frantically ran my fingers through them, attempting to brush them into place.

"I want to see you're all right."

"Really, everything's fine." I tried bending the bangs down.

"I don't know that until I see you. Someone could be making you say that. Open this door now, or I'm coming in."

"Hold your horses." Could've thought of a better phrase than that, considering my embarrassment last night.

I cracked the door open. "See?"

I was the one who saw. Scott in a snug T-shirt and sweatpants. There was no question he worked out.

"All the way open so I know no one is there." His brows were knit together so tightly they must've hurt.

I swung the door open. "Just me."

His face relaxed. I was struck by his concern and felt guilty for not responding more quickly.

"Sorry to be so demanding. I was worried when I heard the loud thud. What happened?"

"Knocked over a chair. Not quite enough room for me to do my exercise routine."

"I'm glad you're fine. I don't know about you, but I could use a cup of coffee. Would you like some?" He headed for the cottage's kitchen.

"Yes, I'd love some. I'll go with you." I touched his back lightly, and he turned. "I feel bad about upsetting you."

"No problem. I'm on edge. After what you told me, it's clear something dangerous is going on. I don't want anything to happen to you."

Other than family, no one had ever said that to me. It felt good to hear.

Helen had left filters and a jar of finely ground coffee next to the coffeepot. I prepared the top compartment as Scott filled the pot with water.

"What do you do for exercise?" He poured water into the coffeemaker.

"I practice tae kwon do, or did, when I was in San Francisco. It's based on what I learned from that."

"What level did you reach?"

Why did I always feel hesitant to tell people? It was one of the most important accomplishments of my life. "Black belt." I didn't look at him. I took a couple of mugs off the hooks on the wall.

Scott let out a low whistle. "Impressive. I know who to hide behind if the going gets tough."

I looked at him, feeling the all-too-familiar warm tingle spread over my face. "We never had to exercise on the ranch. Day-to-day living did it for us from early morning until time for bed. When I left there, I tried workout videos. Not for me. I wanted to do something with a purpose."

Enough coffee had brewed for two cups. He poured it and placed the pot back.

I took a sip of the hot, dark liquid, savoring the smell as much as the strong flavor.

"What about you?" I asked.

"I'm a gym person. It works well, considering the number of hotels I stay at."

I wanted to say it showed. Instead, I checked the clock over the stove. "Helen's starting to put breakfast together. I want to go help her."

"Count me in."

We walked back down the hallway and went into our respective rooms to change clothes. I decided to make life simple and went with black stretch jeans, a white shirt, and my black fleece vest with the silver accents. I fought some more with my hair, added minimal makeup, and headed out.

Scott sat in a brown leather lounge chair in the front room, reading the local paper. "Ready?"

"As much as I'm going to be." I grabbed my coffee mug from the table.

The first rays of sunlight had awakened the birds. Twitters, chirps, and an occasional loud caw from a crow stationed on the whale-shaped wind vane filled the still, moist air. I took a deep breath, relishing the intermingled scents of flowers and the ocean. Early morning was my favorite time with nature.

I tried the handle of the back door of the inn. Locked. Through the window, I saw Helen pulling bowls of fruit from the refrigerator. I knocked.

Helen hurried over and unbolted the door. "Good morning. How did you sleep?"

"Fine. The comforter is scrumptious."

"Glad to hear it." Helen frowned. "Tommy, where are you? You were right behind me a minute ago."

Tommy shuffled into the kitchen, eyes half-closed, hair rumpled, dog-shaped slippers on his feet, velour ears flapping. His pj's were covered with dogs of different shapes and sizes. Fred stumbled along behind him.

"I went to get Fred." He rubbed his knuckles into his eyes. "He was zonked out. I had to shake him to wake him."

"Time for breakfast." She patted the counter, then turned to Scott. "How did you sleep? I kept thinking of you on that little bed with all those animals staring at you."

"No problem. I boned up on my dog breeds and checked out the impressive Lego structures." He chuckled. "It was fun."

Tommy settled himself on a stool, and Scott sat next to him. "I like your pajamas."

I took the place next to Scott.

"As a matter of fact, I saw some similar to those recently, only they had horses on them."

I stepped hard on the toe of his hiking boot. Not enough to hurt, but enough to get his attention.

Scott pulled his foot out from under mine and gave me an impish grin. He turned to Tommy. "I enjoyed all your dog pictures. What kinds of dogs are on your pajamas?"

"I dunno." He looked at them as if for the first time. His eyes opened wider. "This is a golden retriever, and this one is a chocolate lab." He went on identifying each canine. Luckily the pattern repeated itself. "They only show the common breeds. The American Kennel Club recognizes eight hundred and sixty-five breeds. One of the newest ones is the Black Russian Terrier. It was developed by a military kennel named Red Star. It's a combination of rottweiler, giant schnauzer—"

Helen interrupted, "Tommy, Kelly and Scott have a lot to do. I'm sure they appreciate what you're sharing. However, I want you to eat your cereal and then get dressed. It'll be a busy day with the festival going on."

Tommy's eyes flew open. "Yeah. I've heard people talking about all the chocolate treats that'll be there."

"You know you can only have a limited amount. You'll need to choose carefully."

He looked crestfallen. "I know."

"But you can get some samples for another day."

All smiles again. "Thanks, Mom." He grabbed his spoon in the middle of the handle and began to shovel in his cereal.

Helen picked up Fred's dish, opened a covered container by the back door, scooped out two cups of dried dog food, and placed it in the dish. Fred jumped up and down as best he could, considering his short legs and heavy torso.

Helen placed a platter of golden muffins spotted with red raspberries on the counter and bowls of fruit in front of Scott and me. Blueberries mingled with bananas and bright green slices of kiwi fruit in freshly squeezed orange juice.

"Would you like something more? I'd be happy to fix you bacon and eggs."

"This works for me," I said.

Scott had already started on a muffin. "These are delicious. I won't need anything else."

"I'd like to deliver some of the breakfast baskets while Tommy is here with you," Helen said. "Does that work with your plans?"

"You bet." I took a sip of my now-tepid coffee.

"Tommy, I want you to stay with Kelly until I get back."

Tommy mumbled an agreement around a mouthful of cereal. Helen picked up two baskets and left.

Someone knocked on the back door. Scott got up and opened it. "Hi. How can I help you?"

A gangly young man in a red plaid flannel shirt and oil-splattered jeans stood in the doorway.

"I'm Chet Wilson, part of the festival setup crew." He rubbed his hand down the leg of his pants in a futile attempt to clean it and held it out.

Even from a distance the grime under his nails was visible.

Scott shook it without flinching. "Scott Thompson."

Chet shifted his weight back and forth from one foot to the other, his shoulders hunched forward. "We had one of the main tent poles fail during the night. We're trying to find any extra hands so we can get it fixed in time for the event."

"Let me finish a few things here, then I'll be out."

Chet's rocking movement stopped. "Thanks, man. I really appreciate it." He grabbed Scott's hand again and began pumping it vigorously.

Scott extricated his hand. "Happy to be of assistance. We want the chocolate and wine festival to be a success."

"I need to attend to the guests, or I'd help," I said. "We have another person coming in later. I'll send him."

"That's great. Cool." He was now standing a bit straighter, as if pounds of trouble had rolled off his shoulders. "I'll get back to work. See you in a bit." He left at a trot.

Helen came back as Tommy got up and put his bowl in the sink.

"I'm going to get dressed now, Mom."

"Wait." Helen looked at me. "I need to go with him. He can help me deliver baskets when we come back, and we'll be able to get the breakfasts out on time."

"Okay. I'll finish putting them together."

They left, and I prepared the remaining baskets. Scott put dishes in the dishwasher.

"Kelly, I want to speak to you in private for a few minutes," Scott said when we were done. There was no lightness in his tone. "Let's go somewhere where we won't be interrupted."

"Okay." What was up? "We can go in the study."

When we got there, Scott closed the door. "Kelly, I want you to be careful."

"I am. I—"

He put his hand on my shoulder. "I mean it. You're asking questions. This is a small community. Whoever did these things knows you're checking into what's happened."

Goose bumps covered my arms. He was right. I'd already seen how fast information spread through town. Like my poison oak after a night of mindless scratching in my sleep.

"We're backup for each other right now. It's a two-way street. We need to communicate with each other where we are at all times. We're a team. That's what the company rule is about. Protection for staff and guests."

"Right. It makes sense." The goose bumps were still there. "I won't go anywhere without telling you."

He squeezed my shoulder. "Promise?"

It was a fair question. I hadn't exactly followed protocol in Colorado.

"I promise." Our eyes met. I meant it.

Scott let go of my shoulder. "I know you keep your word."

I now had a partner. New concept.

We walked back to the kitchen.

Helen picked up the last couple of breakfast containers. "This will do it." Tommy was next to her, holding a basket, his hair combed back. Fred had been put in his crate by the back door. Mother and son left to finish the morning rounds.

"I'll go see what I can do to help with the tent." Scott headed for the door, but before he could leave, Stanton's cruiser pulled in.

Now what.

The policeman got out, shoving himself up from the driver's seat.

Scott opened the door and waved him in. "I'm Scott Thompson with Resorts International."

"Deputy Sheriff Stanton." He plodded up the stairs.

I saw no spring in his step. "Hi, Deputy Sheriff Stanton."

"Ms. Jackson."

The men shook hands. "Glad to meet you." The deputy walked in. He tossed his hat on the now-familiar counter and slumped down on one of the stools.

The creases in his face were canyons, his eyes the color of a blood-red sunrise. The stubble on his chin was the silver of sagebrush and sure to feel as prickly. "Ms. Jackson, when was the last time you saw Jason Whitcomb?"

I thought for a moment. "It was yesterday afternoon, after the festival committee meeting. Why?"

"He's dead."

Chapter 29

Cupcake man? The one who made Tommy's special treat yesterday? "What happened?"

"Murdered." Deputy Stanton rubbed his sprouting whiskers. "Shot twice. Found next to his van."

"I can't believe it!" I pulled a stool over and sat with a thud.

"Do you know who did it?" Scott asked.

"No. We didn't find anything at the scene that gave us a lead. Maybe something will be discovered during the autopsy or from the evidence we collected."

"Could it be connected with the abalone poaching or the attack on Tommy?" I asked.

"Highly unlikely, Ms. Jackson. There's a lot of drug trafficking in this area. Jason rented a room in a house near the airport. I think he was in the wrong place at the wrong time. Maybe stumbled onto a load of marijuana going out." A network of red blood vessels obliterated the whites of his eyes. He scrunched them closed. "They don't call it the Green Triangle for nothing." Stanton opened his eyes and stretched his back. "Maybe heavier drugs coming in. There's more of that happening now."

Helen bustled in carrying two breakfast baskets, with Tommy close behind. He ran to Fred's crate, knelt down, and let him out. Fred jumped into his arms, grinning from ear to ear. Every wag of his tail shouted, *Where have you been? I've missed you more than you know.* Bringing the joy only a dog could produce time after time in the same day. Tommy hugged him close.

"Good morning, Deputy Sheriff Stanton." Helen placed the baskets on the counter and began to empty them.

"Same to you, Mrs. Rogers."

As Helen unloaded the dishes into the sink, she glanced over at the deputy, studying his face. "Would you like some coffee?"

"Yeah." He stifled a yawn. "That'd be great. Thanks."

Deputy Stanton and I looked at each other, then at Tommy. The unspoken agreement was clear. Don't say anything about the murder.

Helen pulled a mug from a hook under the dish cabinet. "You look exhausted. Have you had anything to eat?" She poured dark, steaming liquid into the cup.

He massaged his forehead. "Sometime last night I grabbed a burger."

"A burger?" Helen stared, her eyebrows raised. "Last night?"

She turned, opened the refrigerator, took out a carton of eggs, and placed it on the counter. "I know I have some cremini mushrooms in here." She put an oversized red bell pepper next to the eggs. "This'll be perfect."

"Please, don't bother, Mrs. Rogers. I'll catch a bite later."

Helen placed a bunch of green onions on the cutting board, the yellow organic label brightly displayed. "Deputy Stanton, you're helping Tommy and me. I want to do something for you in return." She stopped moving and faced the officer. "And I'd feel more comfortable if you called me Helen."

Deputy Stanton looked at her, then away to where Tommy and Fred were playing tug-of-war with a worn rope toy. "Thank you. I'm grateful." He put his large hands around the warm mug. "And please call me Bill."

I wanted to ask more questions, but now wasn't the time for Helen to find out there'd been a murder. Bob's death was still officially an accident. Jason's death wasn't. Jason's was the real deal.

Scott grabbed another muffin from the plate on the counter. "I'm going to go help with the tent."

"I'll be in the study making a call." I nodded at Scott, keeping my agreement with him about letting him know where I was going to be.

He touched the side of his head in a mock salute and flashed a grin.

As I walked down the hallway, questions flew through my mind. What if the deputy was wrong? What if Jason's death was connected? I was convinced Bob was murdered. That would make two murders and one attempted. Jason was off the list for the attack on Tommy because he'd been seen at work during that time, but he could've been involved with the poaching. He could've killed Bob. Or he could've found out something that got him shot.

Tommy was still at risk. I needed to find two people who could've been on the cliff when he was attacked. If there was a connection between the assault on Tommy and Jason's murder, who could've been at the headlands one night and at the place where Jason was killed the next? Phil and Andy provided alibis for each other Wednesday evening, but they could be covering for each other. Where were they last night? And I still didn't know about Charlie.

As soon as I closed the office door, I hurried to the phone and dialed Suzie's number.

"Ralston Hotel," Suzie said in a subdued voice, her usual energy not there.

"Hi. It's Kelly."

"Oh my gosh, did you hear?" Suzie asked. "Someone killed Jason."

The phone lines must be melting.

"Deputy Stanton told me a few minutes ago."

"I can't believe it. We have boxes of pastries he baked for the event today lining the counters." She paused. "It's surreal. His creations are here, and he's gone." Suzie took a deep breath. "He's never coming back."

Never.

That word shot through me.

The finality of it. Someone I saw yesterday and would never see again. I didn't know Bob personally, but I talked to Jason recently. This death was someone in my life. "Did you know him very well?"

"He'd worked here part-time for about eight months. Sweet guy. I really liked him."

"Do you have any idea why someone would kill him? Has he been in any arguments lately?"

"Not that I know of. He baked for us and occasionally helped with catering. He was thorough and conscientious."

Dishes banged in the background. Life went on.

"Bob, Tommy, Jason," Suzie said. "What's going on around here?"

"I thought maybe you'd have an idea because you've been here so long."

"Not a clue."

"Please let me know if you think of anything."

"I will. And, Kelly, be careful. A couple of guys commented on the questions you've been asking."

Warned twice in one morning. Not a good sign. "Thanks for your concern. See you at the festival."

So Suzie didn't know anything, but she was definitely in the information loop. I walked back to the work area.

Helen was in full swing, chopping Italian parsley with vigor. The smell of sautéing onions and bell peppers filled the room. A slab of Parmesan and a grater waited on a counter nearby. Silverware and a napkin were in front of the officer.

"Mrs. Rogers..." Stanton paused. "Helen, I appreciate this." He glanced in my direction. "But I know you have work to do."

"Deputy Stanton, you're working to not only help us, but the community. I'm pleased we have an opportunity to give something to you. Helen's an excellent cook." I smiled. "Her breakfast will give you energy to deal with the day."

"Thanks." The deputy fiddled with his fork and shifted in his chair.

Definitely out of his element. Uncomfortable at being the receiver of good intentions.

Daniel and Allie came in carrying armfuls of flowers.

"Decorations for the tent tables," Daniel stated in answer to my questioning look.

"Where are the vases?" I asked.

Daniel pointed a toe at the cabinets under the counter behind the deputy. "Down there."

"Let me help." Deputy Stanton creaked out of his chair, leaned down, and opened the door. "How many do you need?"

"Five should do it," Daniel said.

He handed the large vases up to me, one at a time.

"Thanks." I placed them on the counter and filled each with water.

Allie and Daniel put the flowers on the counter and began arranging them in the containers.

"Daniel, the setup crew has a problem with one of the poles. I offered your help."

"I'm on it." He turned to his daughter, his long raven hair swinging over his shoulder. "Allie, you're talented at this. Are you okay finishing on your own?"

"You bet, Dad." She beamed up at him, the blue-black locks falling down her back.

Some families resembled each other. Spitting image more closely described these two.

Daniel left and Allie finished arranging the remaining flowers.

"Mom, can we watch television in here?" Tommy asked.

"That's fine." Helen looked at me. "I need to stay here for a while to take care of the dishes and get the afternoon baking started. I've picked up all of the baskets."

Good. Tommy was covered. Nonverbal communication was at an all-time high today.

Tommy and Allie rushed over to the flat-screen television. She picked up the remote, and Tommy pulled out two large green beanbags from against the wall. They flopped down in them, and Fred squeezed in between the two of them, settling with a contented grunt.

Helen flipped one side of the omelet over her mixture of herbs, vegetables, and cheese and gently slid it out of the pan onto a warmed plate. She garnished it with some finely chopped tomato and dill sprigs. Placing it on a tray, she added a cup of fresh fruit, then put it in front of the deputy, along with a basket of thick-sliced homemade wheat bread.

Deputy Stanton shoveled a few forkfuls in like a starving trucker after a long haul on a barren stretch of road. He suddenly stopped, sheepishly glanced at us, then slowly filled his fork and took another bite.

He smiled at Helen. "I was hungrier than I thought, and you make an amazing breakfast."

"Thank you." Helen busied herself at the sink. "Glad I was able to help."

"I'm going to the office to do some paperwork." I headed back down the hallway.

I spent a couple of hours taking care of orders and invoices, pushing thoughts of Jason out of my mind. I stopped at eleven thirty. Time to see how the festival was going . . . and to think about who could've killed Jason.

The huge festival tent covered scores of tables filled with wine, chocolate goodies, and gifts for the silent auction. I saw Scott and headed in his direction. He waved, holding what appeared to be a cupcake.

"Is the pole taken care of?" I asked.

"Yes. And the tasting has begun." He grinned.

A dark fudge-like frosting and some kind of cream filling surrounded by cake disappeared into his mouth.

I felt a tug on my sleeve.

"Miss Kelly, could I talk to you for a minute?" Tommy asked, his eyes wide.

"Sure." I wondered what was up.

"I want to go somewhere private." He was all serious in tone.

"Okay. Let's go to the far end where the roses are."

Daniel observed us from a few feet away.

"Tommy and I are going to have a chat. I'll bring him back to you when we're done."

"Got it," Daniel said.

I looked at Scott. "We'll be at the end of the tents and will stay in sight."

He nodded and his hand reached out for a chocolate truffle decorated with white chocolate stars. "I'll be here."

Tommy and I walked to where the yellow fragrant flowers had attracted Mary when she was on her Silver Sentinel shift to watch the inn.

"I didn't tell you everything the other night." Tears began to flow. "I know I can only have Fred here if he's good." He squatted down and clutched the thick-necked dog.

I'd known there was more. "Tommy, what happened?"

"Miss Kelly, please don't make me get rid of Fred. Please," he sobbed.

His nose needed a tissue.

"Please, I can't lose him," he wailed. High-pitched. Heartbreaking. The tears were a river.

What on earth had the dog done?

Chapter 30

"Tommy, I know Fred's a good dog. You won't have to get rid of him."

"Honest?" Tommy's eyes were hopeful, the beginning of a smile appeared. "But you don't know what he did yet." The corners of his mouth drooped.

"Please tell me what happened." I held my breath. Had the dog done something terrible? Had I just made a false promise?

"He . . . he . . . chased Mrs. Henderson's cat." Fear controlled every inch of his body and contorted his face.

I exhaled. I wanted to laugh with relief.

My father's voice called to me from years ago. *"Erase your face. Show no emotion."* Advice he'd given when I was handling my first difficult ranch guest. Laughing would devastate Tommy right now. I couldn't make light of something so serious to him.

"Did he injure the cat?"

"No. It got away."

"Please tell me the whole story."

Tommy stood. "I took Fred with me when I went to the post office for Mom after school on Wednesday." He looked down and began making circles in the grass with the toe of his worn red sneaker.

"And?" I prompted.

"I let Fred off his leash in the field nearby so I could throw a ball for him." The toe circled faster, wearing a groove in the grass. "I know I'm not supposed to. I promise I'll never do it again. Ever." His eyes met mine.

"I believe you. Then what?"

"Mrs. Henderson's orange tabby cat jumped out of the grass

under Fred's nose, and he started chasing it." His eyes wandered to the tables under the large tent.

"And . . ." I prompted again.

He sighed. "He ran across Mrs. Smith's backyard. She was hanging up clothes to dry." Tommy studied me warily, as if scared to add more wrongs to Fred's list of offenses. "He knocked over her laundry basket."

"Was she upset?"

"I don't know. I didn't stop. I was running after Fred as fast as I could." He looked at the dog. "We went back later and apologized. She said nothing got dirty and everything was okay."

I pulled a clean tissue out of my pocket and handed it to him.

"What happened next?"

"Fred ran past the post office and across the street and squeezed under a fence. I opened a gate and followed him. The man who gave me the cupcake was loading stuff into his van."

Jason. "What kind of stuff?"

"Big bags." He shoved the tissue into his pocket. "I chased Fred to the other side of the yard, and he went under the fence again. I opened another gate and ran out. I found him sniffing around and put a leash on him. The cat had disappeared."

"Did you see what was in the bags?"

"No, but I tripped on one. There were big, hard things in them. They felt like rocks."

What could be described as big rocks that were being loaded into a van in large bags? Abalone.

"Did Jason, the man who gave you the cupcake, see you?"

"Probably. He had his back to me when I ran in, but the yard's pretty big, and Fred was baying by the time we got to the back of it."

"Tommy, I think you learned a lot from this experience." I touched him lightly on the shoulder. "You can keep Fred."

Tommy jumped up and down, clapping his hands. "Thank you! Thank you!"

Fred jumped up and down, too, never one to miss a good time. Little did he know he'd just been spared.

"Thank you for telling me about Wednesday. Fred's a wonderful dog. He just didn't resist temptation that day."

Daniel and Allie waved in the distance.

Allie came running up, a chocolate something in her hand. "Tommy, you have to try the chocolate mousse brownies. They are soo . . . good." She rolled her eyes.

Daniel strolled up beside her. "She's right." He looked at me. "The chefs in the area plan for months to come up with unusual chocolate delectables."

Allie handed part of her brownie to Tommy.

"Thanks!" The chocolate disappeared in one bite.

Daniel turned to me. "He's staying with Allie and me until Helen can join us."

"Miss Kelly, can I go now?"

"You bet. Have fun sampling."

Tommy grinned, and the three of them walked off with Fred in tow. The kids stopped at the first table, and their hands darted out for chocolate cookies.

I walked through the tented area, passing numerous tables of wine and sweets, in search of Scott and thinking about what I'd learned. Jason. How could the man who made mothers want to pinch his cheeks be involved with poaching?

"Would you like to try some truffles?" A young woman wearing a black wool sweater patterned with several varieties of colorful flowers gestured toward her display of candy.

Startled out of my thoughts, I stopped.

A display of mini-truffles was before me.

"Please, help yourself." Amy, her name tag read.

Maybe it'll stimulate my brain and I can figure this whole thing out.

"Thanks." I placed one in my mouth, letting it slowly melt. The intense chocolate was heaven. Scott stood a couple of tables away, next to a fountain of dripping chocolate, and I headed in his direction.

"Hi," Scott said. "Have you tried any goodies yet?"

"Yes. The truffles are luscious. Scott, Tommy told me something—"

Just then, Andy came huffing up to us. "Suzie's table is almost out of pastries. She left a while ago to get some. Could one of you find out where she is?"

"Probably got pulled into some hotel business," Scott said.

"I'll go." Perfect. I could check out where Tommy had seen Jason. "It's only a couple of blocks away. I should be back in a heartbeat."

Scott frowned but didn't say anything as I walked away.

Up one block, I turned left. Tommy said the fenced lot was across from the post office. I could walk through it, and I'd be only a short distance from Suzie's place.

The cool ocean breeze streamed through my hair as I strode down the wooden boardwalk. It was empty, and I walked fast.

Jason had been involved in the poaching operation. He smuggled them out in his catering van. The location Tommy had talked about was where the boy had seen Andy and Charlie on Thursday.

Could the three of them have been in it together? Andy and Charlie could've been the two who were there the night of Tommy's attack. But that would mean Phil was in on it, too. He gave Andy an alibi. And why kill Jason? My head was spinning.

And silver and gold. Where did that fit in? Charlie's car was silver, Andy's was gold, and Jason's was white. If the colors meant anything, that could put Charlie and Andy together, but Jason was the one with the abalone. It all didn't add up.

I spied the post office up the street on my right. There was only one fence that fit the location Tommy described. The wood was gray with age and beaten by the elements. I lifted the worn latch and let myself in. The lot was empty, except for rusty pieces of a sink tossed in one corner.

Tommy said Jason was putting the bags in the truck. Why was he loading the sacks here? Where had they come from?

I walked slowly toward the other side, scanning the ground, and found an area where the grass was flattened a bit. I bent down, searching carefully, hoping to find something. Nothing. Why didn't real life happen like on television? A convenient clue popping up would be nice.

I went to the far end and opened the gate that had eventually led to Tommy's reunion with Fred. Suzie's storage shed was two buildings down on the right. The door to it was closed. Charlie's truck was parked outside. He was a suspect. I broke into a run. Was Suzie alone with Charlie? Was she in danger?

Chapter 31

I raced toward the storage building.

What was Charlie doing there?

Delivering water? No. It was Saturday.

Where was Suzie?

Forget polite knocking. I twisted the knob and pushed the door open.

Charlie was sprawled on his side on the floor. Suzie crouched beside him, one hand on his shoulder.

"Suzie, are you okay?" I ran up to her.

As she turned, a huge metal wrench gleamed in her hand.

The expression on her face reminded me of the bobcat I surprised in the barn one winter, hunched over a slaughtered goat. The predator's lips had been curled back in a defiant snarl. Its eyes shifted from side to side, seeking escape, then back to me. Trapped.

I froze.

"Suzie, what happened? Are . . . are . . . you okay?" I stammered.

A trickle of blood glistened on Charlie's cheek. There was no movement. He was unconscious . . . or dead.

She rose slowly, her eyes never leaving me. "It's my third strike. I won't go back," she uttered between clenched teeth. "I won't."

Suzie moved to my left. Before I realized what she was doing, she had cut me off from the door. She came toward me, the heavy tool at her side, a red stain along its edge.

"I didn't want to hurt anybody, but I won't go back."

"What are you talking about? Go back where? And what's a third strike?" I slowly began to back into the storage shelves. My peripheral vision worked overtime trying to find something I could use to defend myself.

"Prison, that's where. I'm in for life with a third offense." The wrench began to rise. "I'd rather die."

Life in prison. She'd rather die. There was nothing for her to lose if she killed me.

I stumbled back another step and grabbed a wire shelf. Industrial-sized olive oil cans were stacked next to my hand.

She approached, wrench held high, gripping it with both hands.

Keep her talking. "Did you kill Bob?"

Suzie stopped. "He found out I was involved with the abalone poaching and wanted me to turn myself in. Get a lighter sentence." She stared at me with eyes devoid of emotion. "I told him I wouldn't go back to jail. He said he was sorry, but he had to do what was right. I grabbed his arm and begged, but he insisted he had to report it." Her shoulders sagged. "I shoved him. I was so scared, so angry."

"Suzie, you didn't plan to kill him. It wasn't premeditated." I darted a quick glance at the bottles and cans on the shelves. "That makes a difference."

"His wasn't deliberate, but Jason's was." Suzie took a step forward. "He planned on splitting and tried to blackmail me over Bob's death. I knew he'd always be a threat."

A shaft of sunlight hit a strand of Suzie's hair. Gold. Jason's prematurely gray hair. Silver. The words the Sentinels had decoded. Now it all made sense.

She lunged at me, swinging the wrench downward.

I seized one of the large cans of olive oil by the handle, held it up, and blocked the blow. The clashing sound of metal on metal made my ears ring. I staggered under the fierce power of the hit and went down on one knee. Pain shot through my wrist.

Suzie swung again.

Another crushing blow. The can buckled. She raised the wrench upward, but before she could swing again, I thrust the container into her legs.

She staggered, and the tool aimed for my head came down on the can, puncturing it. Oil spewed out. I stepped backward; Suzie came forward, then began slipping in the greasy liquid. It was like some macabre dance—bloodied wrench and dancing feet.

Suzie began to fall. She clutched a wire shelf with one hand to stay upright.

I leapt for the wrench.

She struck out at me and missed. The momentum of the heavy weapon pulled it out of her hand and sent it flying.

Suzie let go of her support and grabbed the front of my fleece vest with both hands. She yanked me toward her. My feet hit the oil. I clutched her jacket. We began to slide like ice-skaters out of control. We held on to each other in an embrace of death. If I let go, I could die.

Her hands released me for an instant and then they were around my throat.

I lost my balance, and we crashed to the floor. The impact broke her grip.

We rolled over and over—grabbing, hitting, slapping. My head hit the concrete as Suzie managed to slam me downward. Pain blasted through my forehead. I pushed her over, caught a handful of hair, and pulled her head back. Suzie raked my face with her fingernails.

She locked a foot onto the end of the wire shelf; her body went stiff, stopping our movement. Suzie shoved, and I slid.

She got to her knees. The wrench was a couple of feet away. As she reached for it, I launched myself forward and into her, knocking her backward. Her head grazed a metal shelf.

Suzie fell back and blinked a few times. She didn't move.

But I did. With shaking fingers, I unbuckled my belt and ripped it off. I turned her over and cinched her hands together behind her back.

She began to struggle, but the knot held.

I hunched over, my head in my hands, gasping for air. Straightening up, there were red smears on my hands. I gingerly touched my throbbing temple. There'd be a humdinger of a bump.

The door burst open. Fran and two male game wardens ran into the room, guns raised.

"Is there anyone else here?" Fran barked at me.

"I don't know."

"I'll check." One of the men headed behind the shelving area. The other one hurried to Charlie, calling for an ambulance on his cell phone.

Fran approached me. "Are you okay?"

"I think so. Careful. That's oil on the floor."

Her boot was ready to land in a pool of it.

"Trust me, I know how slippery it is."

Sirens rapidly got louder.

Fran did a quick survey of the room and went over to where towels hung next to a large sink. She took them and covered the oil on the floor. Ignoring Suzie, she knelt down next to me.

She leaned in and examined my injury. "How do you feel? Are you nauseated?"

"No." I knew the routine questions. I'd fallen off horses enough times. "I've been through the concussion questions before. I don't have any of the symptoms."

Fran nodded. "Good." She turned to look at Charlie.

I saw faint stirrings.

"He's coming to," said the man kneeling next to him.

A moan heralded Charlie's return to the living.

"Everything is clear back here," said the warden who'd checked the back area.

A deafening siren suddenly stopped. Doors slammed, and a familiar voice yelled, "Stay there and keep people out."

Deputy Sheriff Stanton plunged through the door, gun drawn.

"It's all under control," Fran said immediately.

He lowered his gun.

Someone shouted, "Kelly, are you in there? Are you okay?"

Scott.

I grabbed a shelf and pulled myself to my feet.

"Are you sure you should be doing that?" Fran asked.

No. "Yes. I'll be fine." I hobbled to a window, careful to stay on the towels Fran had put down. I struggled with the latch and was finally able to crack the warped wood open an inch. It was enough.

"Scott, I'm okay. I'll be out in a bit." With that, I sank to the floor, my head pounding.

Another siren stopped. Two paramedics, kits in hand, rushed through the door. One went to Charlie, and one hurried to me, carefully following Fran's towel trail.

He knelt down beside me. "Let me look."

The medic gently examined my wound and then my entire head. "Lucky. I only see one small cut and some scrapes."

"Nothing like a good can of olive oil to keep you healthy." My pathetic attempt at a joke. Either that or cry. What a fool I'd been. I'd trusted Suzie so completely.

"Do you hurt anywhere else?" He opened his case.

"No. I'm trembling, but that's the adrenaline."

"Understandable." He cleaned the area on my forehead. "We always recommend people go to the hospital after a head injury to get checked out."

"I'll have someone take me over."

He snapped his case shut. A warden and the other paramedic were taking Charlie out the door on a stretcher.

I grasped the window ledge and began to haul myself up. This was beginning to be a habit.

"Let me help you." He supported me as I stood, then he went to Suzie.

Fran came over. "We all want to thank you."

"For what?" Getting beaten up by Suzie?

"Charlie's one of us. He's been working undercover. He'd be dead if you hadn't shown up. We're grateful." The grizzled woman turned away as tears showed in the corners of her eyes. She grabbed a handkerchief out of her pocket and wiped her eyes. Visible emotion gone.

Charlie. An officer of the law. How far off was I on that one.

"How did you know we were here?"

"He radioed in he had a suspect in the abalone poaching ring. Charlie gave us her name and location and said she was packing her car with personal possessions. He figured she was fleeing." Fran shook her head. "We got here as fast as we could. It's a big county."

"I demand to be let in!" an authoritative voice came through the flimsy walls. "One of my employees is in there. It's my responsibility to take care of her."

Corrigan. Not great timing.

"Do you see a mirror around here? Or do you have one?"

Fran gave me a funny look. "Uh . . . I haven't seen one." She paused. "And maybe you don't want one right now."

What was that supposed to mean? The tough, no-nonsense game warden was looking at me like I was Medusa.

Nothing to be done about it. I ran my fingers through my hair, feeling greasy, matted strands. I wiped my face with a corner of my once-white shirt and saw a dirty smear with a little blood mixed in. Straightening my shoulders, I marched out—or more like tottered.

Corrigan stood outside the door, looming over a tall deputy who blocked his way. He was about to say something when he saw me. His mouth remained open, but he said nothing.

Uh-oh. That bad. I should've known from Fran's reaction. Tommy and Fred were next to him. I didn't think Tommy's eyes could get any bigger than I'd seen them, but they did. Even Fred looked serious.

"I'm okay. Really. If something was really wrong, they'd have sent me off in the ambulance. You don't have to worry about . . ." I was rattling on.

"Kelly, breathe." Scott walked up next to me and put an arm around my shoulders.

Oh. Breathing.

Fran approached Corrigan. "Are you Kelly's employer?"

"Yes." Corrigan's tone was subdued.

"I'm Warden Fran Cartwright." She thrust her hand out to Corrigan and they shook. "Kelly saved the life of one of our officers. She's one tough cookie. We're all deeply grateful to her."

"Thanks for telling me that." Corrigan looked in my direction. "She means a lot to us."

Chapter 32

The next morning I awoke in my room at the inn with more painful muscles than I'd ever had before, and that was saying a lot after growing up on a ranch. I stretched one limb at a time. They all responded way too vocally in terms of pain.

I threw back the covers and walked stiffly over to the coffeemaker. Thank you, Corrigan, for your devotion to superb java. Smelling the ground beans was the beginning of revival.

The aroma of freshly brewed coffee greeted me as I stepped out of the shower. Wonderful! But what I saw in the mirror was a different kind of hello. The beginning of a black eye made me look like a one-eyed raccoon. Good thing my sister was into makeup and insisted I carry supplies when I packed in a hurry.

I toweled off, dressed, and did my usual routine with extra eye time. Yesterday's events churned through my mind like a movie on fast-forward. The fight. The hospital. A tired Scott saying good night and leaving for the company retreat. The smell of frying bacon filled the hallway as I walked toward the kitchen.

Helen glanced up from stirring a pan full of scrambled eggs. "Good morning. How do you feel?"

"Creaky, but walking."

She laughed. "Well, maybe we can oil your joints with some good food." Helen turned off the burner. "Scott called. He should be here any minute."

Oil. Right. I rubbed the bump on my head.

As if on cue, Scott opened the door and walked in. "Kelly, how are you?"

I smiled. "A little sore, but fine."

Helen added sautéed red and green bell peppers, onions, mushrooms, and a generous pinch of fresh herbs to the eggs and piled them onto two plates. She placed homemade wheat toast and bacon next to them. I could get used to this.

Silverware and napkins were already on the counters. "Dig in." She put the meal in front of us.

And that we did. It had been a long twenty-four hours.

"Scott, thanks for taking me to the emergency room yesterday," I said between mouthfuls. The wait, the tests, and the examinations had taken hours. Dinner never happened.

"You're welcome." He was devouring his breakfast.

We ate in dedicated silence for a few minutes.

"Where's Tommy?" I asked.

"Enjoying his newfound freedom," Helen replied. "He's outside playing with Fred."

"I'm sure happy it's all over." My shoulders slumped, emotional exhaustion dragging them down.

Scott pushed his plate back. "Thanks for the terrific breakfast, Helen. That'll help see me through the day."

"You're welcome. All of you have done so much to help Tommy and me. I appreciate it." She picked up his dish. "It's the least I can do."

Scott turned to me. "Corrigan should be arriving shortly. He wants us all to meet in the conference room. He's invited the Silver Sentinels."

The Silver Sentinels? What was that about? "Okay. I'll be ready."

Scott's cell phone rang, and he stepped outside to answer it.

I headed back to my room to check my blossoming black eye. I put on a little more makeup and headed for the conference room, where Bob's accident had first been declared a murder.

The group was there. In deference to breakfast, Mary had brought croissants, dark purple fruit oozing from the ends. I sat next to the Professor. The fragrance of his aftershave drifted through the air. Ivan rubbed at a nicked area on his chin—a hazard from shaving. Rudy placed one of Mary's treats on a small plate. Gertie sat up straight, pen and notepad ready.

What a wonderful group of people. I was so fortunate to have met them.

Tommy and Fred bounded in, followed by Corrigan and Helen.

"Hey, everyone." Fran entered with Deputy Sheriff Stanton behind her.

Helen had already put water pitchers and glasses on the table.

Mugs were on top of a back cabinet, with two large thermoses of coffee next to them. Plates, silverware, and napkins were on the counter, along with a basket heaped with muffins. She'd been busy this morning.

"Fran, how is Charlie?" I asked.

"He'll be fine. He has to stay put in the hospital for a while, though." She laughed. "That will be real torture for him. He's always on the go."

Corrigan shifted in his chair. "I want to thank you all for meeting with me today and helping to bring closure to the recent tragic events. Please, tell me what happened from the beginning."

I listened as each person shared their thoughts and actions. I chimed in as appropriate. The story was told.

"I can add some new information." Deputy Sheriff Stanton pushed his coffee mug back and put his elbows on the table. "Suzie told us everything. She had nothing to lose and maybe some small consideration to be gained. Suzie partnered with Jason. She let him store the abalone in the refrigerators at the hotel."

I shook my head, still stunned by the turn of events.

"Bob knew Jason was poaching but didn't know where such a large amount of abalone was being kept between his trips to San Francisco. When Bob visited Suzie on the day he died, he encountered Jason and suspected Suzie was his accomplice."

"Who attacked Tommy?" asked Gertie.

I realized they didn't know everything that happened. It seemed like ages ago that Tommy shared Fred's escapade.

"Jason attempted to toss Tommy off the cliff because he saw him loading bags of abalone into his van," the deputy said.

All eyes turned to the boy.

Tommy sat on the floor in the corner of the room, staring at the dog lounging in his lap. He gently tugged on Fred's long ears.

"Suzie stopped him. Bob's death wasn't planned. She panicked." Stanton sighed. "Killing Tommy would've been cold-blooded murder. She wouldn't allow that. She has a streak of decency in her."

"What about Jason's murder?" I asked.

"She told Jason what happened to Bob. They didn't know how much information he had collected or where it was. Hence Bob's stolen phone." Deputy Stanton shot me a look. "Suzie heard your phone conversation and knew where Helen put it. She saw you talking to the kids and got to the inn before you."

Ha! I was right about it being connected.

"Jason decided to run. He demanded she meet him and bring money."

"Ah . . . good old-fashioned blackmail." The Professor nodded his head. "Fear and greed weighed in here. Basic emotions lie at the bottom of most murders."

"Suzie wasn't sure what she was going to do. She took what money she could gather together and a gun that had belonged to her husband." He shrugged. "Jason said thanks and he'd be in touch for more. Then she pulled the gun. They fought. She shot."

"Thanks for telling us. I'm glad we can bring closure to Bob's death," Corrigan said.

The silence lengthened. Everyone seemed to be examining their fingernails. Fred stood up and yawned.

Corrigan called out, "Hey, Fred, come here, boy."

The low-slung hound walked over to Corrigan.

He ruffled his ears. "This is the one who failed his final exam at the cancer clinic?"

"Yeah," Tommy said.

"Bob told me about him."

"They asked us if we wanted him because he couldn't be one of their cancer detection dogs," Tommy said.

"*Nyet!* Enough!" Ivan roared. "This is great dog. Is wrong people don't know." He scowled as Mary grabbed his arm.

"We all promised," she pleaded.

"Ivan, no!" Rudy implored, tugging on Ivan's other arm.

"What do you mean?" I asked.

"He smell cancer. Like trained." Ivan glared defiantly at the others.

"How do you know?" I asked.

The Professor let out a deep sigh. "We take Fred when we go on visits to nursing homes. He's a certified therapy dog."

Gertie piped up. "We saw that with certain patients he put his paw on their knee. We didn't think anything of it at first."

"One of the people told me she'd been diagnosed with cancer," Mary said. "I saw Fred put his paw on her knee when we entered the room."

Mary grabbed one of her breakfast pastries and took several quick bites.

We all waited to hear more.

She looked at a corner of the ceiling, avoiding eye contact. "I had another person tell me the same thing that day, and Fred put his paw on that person's knee, as well."

"When Mary told us her story, we began comparing notes," the Professor said.

Rudy chimed in. "We believe Fred can detect cancer. He just doesn't signal it the way he was taught."

"We not say anything," Ivan rumbled. "We not want boy to lose dog. Maybe he have to go back to clinic." He clasped his work-worn hands together. "We not want to lose dog, either."

"There's no problem there," Helen said. "Tommy's named as sole owner on his papers."

I swear five pairs of stiff shoulders dropped simultaneously and five grins appeared.

"So . . . if Fred puts his paw on a person's knee, that means they have cancer?" Tommy asked.

"Appears that way," the Professor said.

Tommy stood and began to back away. "No," he shouted, an expression of horror on his face.

Fear shot through me. "Tommy, what is it?"

He looked at me with wild eyes and raced from the room, Fred on his heels.

I followed, a fleeting vision of bewildered looks from the group in my mind. I grabbed the truck keys and a fleece from a hook by the door and ran to the Toyota.

Pulling out of the driveway, I caught a glimpse of Tommy cutting across the adjacent field on his bike. As I watched, he began to ascend a steep hill, the bike lurching from side to side as he struggled to make it to the top. Fred followed. The two disappeared over the crest.

I didn't want to stop him. I wanted to see where he was going. And I didn't want to lose him. I pushed the gas pedal down.

As I reached the top, Tommy bounced his way down a dirt path to my left, through an empty lot. Not able to follow in the pickup, I stopped and took binoculars out of the glove box.

Tommy turned into a driveway, dropped his bike, and ran up to the front door of a house. He pounded on it.

I recognized the VW bus parked next to the home.

Daniel opened the door.

Tears streamed down Tommy's face. I couldn't hear him, but I could read his lips.

"Where's Allie?" he mouthed.

Daniel opened the door wider, and Tommy pushed past, followed by Fred.

I put the binoculars down, put the truck in gear, and drove to the home via a more roundabout way.

I pulled into the driveway, turned the vehicle off, and paused for a minute. I was scared what this might mean. I dreaded telling Daniel.

It had to be done. I took several deep breaths, got out, and walked to the door. I raised my hand and hesitated. Then I gave a couple of sharp raps.

It took Daniel a couple of minutes to answer. "Kelly, thank goodness you're here. What's wrong with Tommy? He's crying so hard, he can't speak."

"Daniel, we need to talk."

Chapter 33

The buzz of the alarm jarred me into consciousness once again. Yesterday's events filtered sluggishly through my half-awake mind. Fred could detect cancer. Michael had flown Allie and Daniel to Beacon Medical Center. They'd discovered a melanoma, but she would be fine. It had been caught at an early stage. Scott had been sent away on a "burning fire" mission, as he called it.

I pulled the down comforter over my head. Just a few more minutes of warmth, softness, and quiet. It felt good to be back home in my own bed.

Home? In my own bed? Where did that come from? Had I really connected that much to Redwood Cove? I flipped the comforter back and stared at the ceiling. What wasn't to like about the place? A small town on a beautiful coast. That worked for me. I was a small-town girl. I learned that after the brief time I spent in a couple of big cities. I thought of the Silver Sentinels. Friends helping friends. I liked that, too. I felt comfortable here. I hoped I had a chance to come back to Redwood Cove in the future.

Sighing, I knew I couldn't ignore the new day anymore. I rolled out of bed and winced. My sore muscles needed time to warm up. I walked to the kitchenette, started the coffee, headed for the shower, and began the whole getting-ready routine. After I finished, I took a couple of aspirin and put the bottle in the pocket of my fleece vest.

I entered the work area, my cup clutched in my right hand.

I stopped. A man wearing a gray pin-striped suit stood looking out the back door. The razor-cut line of hair on the back of his neck would make a general proud.

"May I help you?" I asked, bewildered by a stranger in our private area.

He turned around.

"Daniel?" Was I dreaming? "What . . . Why . . ." I stopped, speechless.

"Good morning, Kelly." He raised an eyebrow. "What do you think?"

"I . . . uhhh . . . you look great," I stammered. "I mean . . . not that you didn't look great, uhh, nice before . . . I thought you looked wonderful." My face felt on fire. I was getting in deeper and deeper. "It's a different look," I finally managed to say.

Daniel laughed. "Thanks for all the compliments . . . I think."

"Would you like some coffee?"

"Yes, thanks." Daniel settled himself on a stool.

"Why the suit?" I handed him a mug.

"I decided to apply for Bob's job. I want to be a better provider for Allie." He paused. "And it's time for me to make some changes in my life."

"That's wonderful, Daniel." But did he have any experience running a place like this?

"I majored in business management before I dropped out of college."

A shiver raced down my spine. I felt like he'd read my mind.

"I thought about it during the flight back yesterday and asked Corrigan if I could meet with him. We have an interview scheduled here in about fifteen minutes."

I knew Michael was only here a couple of days. Quick thinking on Daniel's part.

"I got in touch with a couple of buddies, and they found the suit and shoes and cut my hair." He grimaced. "I don't remember my neck ever feeling so cold!"

He got up and fetched a worn leather briefcase leaning against the wall. He pulled out some papers and handed them to me.

"I won't tell you how many years I've had this." He held up the portfolio. "It lived in the back of the closet from the day I moved here until yesterday."

His résumé's format was outdated, but the critical information was there. Impressive that he'd pulled it all together so quickly.

"Daniel, I wish you the best. If Michael asks me how it's been working with you, rest assured I'll only have wonderful things to say."

Crunching gravel heralded Corrigan's arrival. Through the back window we saw him pull up in the black Mercedes and park next to the pickup.

Daniel took a deep breath and straightened his shoulders.

"You'll do fine." I handed the résumé back to him.

"Thanks, Kelly." He placed the papers back in his leather case.

Corrigan opened the door and stopped. He blinked a few times. "Hi, Daniel. Looks like you're ready for the interview."

"Yes, sir."

I thought he was going to salute.

"Kelly, how are you doing today?" Corrigan asked.

"Fine," I lied. "A little more coffee and my batteries will be charged for the day."

"Glad to hear it. Is there a problem with me using the office right now?"

"No. I'll be taking care of guests. Helen came in early to do breakfast. I told her last night to take the rest of the day off after that. I'll take care of the finished breakfast baskets. She's been working extra hours since Bob died, and I thought she'd like some quiet time with Tommy."

Michael looked at me thoughtfully. "Good idea."

The two of them headed for the office while I poured more dark, hot liquid from a thermos Helen had prepared. We only had three guests left. Checking them out would be easy. Easy. I liked the sound of that right now.

As I sat down at the counter and sipped the hot brew, my cell phone rang. I checked the number. Scott.

"Hey, how are you doing? I got your message about an emergency. Where did you end up going?"

"I'm in stunning Sedona with a miserable twerp of a real estate agent."

"Fun and not so fun, it sounds like. I love Sedona."

"You've been here before?"

"Several times. Be sure you get up to the Red Rim Café at the airport. With any luck, they still have the all-you-can-eat crab feeds."

I stopped. I realized I didn't really know much about Scott. It was a very basic restaurant frequented by families and people grabbing a bite to eat after work. I thought of his immaculate clothes and quality leather shoes. All I had seen him in until recently.

"Though it might not be what you're used to. It's not fancy," I added hastily. "Mostly locals."

"I'm not about fancy, Kelly. Good food and good company are what interest me." He paused. "I wish you could be here to show me around and share that delicious-sounding dinner."

"Maybe we can do that sometime." Did I really say that? I'd promised I wasn't getting involved with anyone.

"We have a company retreat in a few months. I'll see you then, if not before."

"I look forward to it." My fluttering heart didn't seem to be in agreement with my reservations.

"Kelly, let's stay in touch. We have very isolating jobs."

"I'd like that, too." Where was this going?

"There are a lot of issues and ideas that come up when I'm out in the field. Bouncing them off of someone would be great. It's nice having someone to talk to."

Oh, business.

"And not just about business," Scott said.

What was up today? Was I thinking out loud?

"I enjoyed getting to know you on a more personal basis."

"I learned some new things about you, too." Like the jeans and hiking shoes.

"Gotta go. And don't let anything happen to those horse pajamas. Very cute. 'Bye."

He hung up before I could get in a retort. I sipped the coffee, thinking I was already looking forward to the next time we talked.

The finished breakfast baskets were outside the guest rooms. Back in the kitchen, I placed them on the counter. I toasted some bread and spread it with organic peanut butter and homemade wild strawberry jam. I took a couple of bites and began to put dishes in the sink.

I heard men's voices in the hallway. Michael and Daniel entered.

"Welcome aboard." Michael gave Daniel a hearty clap on the back.

"Thank you, sir."

"No more 'sir.' My staff calls me Michael."

"I won't let you down." Daniel turned to me. "Kelly, do you need me for anything today?"

"No." This was his usual day off. "It's a good time for you and Allie to be together." I smiled at him. "And congratulations."

He beamed and hurried out the door.

"It's been quite the few days for you." Michael sat down on one of the stools.

"Yep. Do you want some coffee?"

"Sounds good. You know me."

I chose a large mug, filled it, and handed it to him. I walked around the counter and sat beside him.

"I'm glad you came out of it okay. Your father would've never forgiven me." He took a sip of his coffee.

"Michael, this was my first assignment as an administrator for your company. I'd like your feedback on how I did."

"You did an excellent job. You stepped into an unknown situation, followed company protocol, and used your ingenuity to solve a crime."

"Thanks."

"More than that, you valued the people of the community and the employees. You respected the Silver Sentinels. Some people would've dismissed them. You supported Helen and Tommy, putting them first. Giving them your room. Filling in today." He paused. "That's what I want from people in this company—thinking in a big-picture way. It's a sense of family and working together I want to create. You've done that. Your dad will be proud."

"Thank you for the compliments." I turned the mug around and around in my hands. "I know you and Dad are friends and that's why I got considered for the job as a temporary assistant in Colorado."

"Right." Corrigan looked puzzled.

"Michael, it's important for me to be appreciated for myself as an individual and what I can contribute."

Corrigan straightened up on the stool.

I looked at him. "Do I have this job as an executive administrator because of who I am and what I did in Colorado or because of your friendship with my father?"

He was quiet for a moment.

"You earned it every bit of the way." He leaned toward me. "I mean that. It has nothing to do with your father."

I took a deep breath. "Thank you. That means a lot."

"You're right about my giving you some special consideration when I hired you in the beginning. I knew about your upbringing and what you did on the ranch. Making you an executive administrator was my decision based on your performance. And what you accomplished here shows me I did the right thing."

"Thanks for telling me that."

"You're one of us. You're part of the team." He gave me a quick hug. "I have some business I need to attend to today. I'd like to meet tomorrow morning and talk about Daniel taking over."

"Okay."

"Unfortunately, I'll have to start searching for another manager in a month or so."

I sat up, confused. "What do you mean?" He'd just hired Daniel.

"The Ridley House came on the market. I've been wanting to buy and renovate it for years. I'm meeting with the real estate agent today to put in an offer."

"So you'll be looking for a manager for the new place?"

"No, I'm going to assign Daniel to it. I know he refers to himself as a handyman, but he's much more than that. He's a very skilled carpenter. Daniel also spent a lot of time working for a contractor whom I know and respect. It's going to need a lot of work. Daniel can oversee the job and do some of the work himself. I'm sending one of my architects out to prepare the plans."

"Does that mean you'll be looking for a manager for this place?" My thoughts flew back to this morning. Thoughts of home.

"Yep. Back to square one."

"Michael"—I swallowed hard—"I'd like to be the manager here."

Corrigan put his cup on the counter and stared at me. "Are you saying you'd like to move here and make this your full-time job?"

I took in a deep breath. Was I sure? "Yes." The answer rang true in my heart of hearts.

"This is a very small town, a place where it can take a long time to develop friendships."

"I feel I already have some friends. And a small town is what I like, it's where I belong." My excitement was building.

"I was going to give you a choice of two different resorts for your next assignment—one in the Bahamas and one in Florida."

I didn't feel the slightest interest. "I'd like to stay here."

"Okay. I'm willing to let you give it a try on one condition."

"What's that?"

"If it doesn't work out, you let me know. Don't let pride get in the way. You can have your current position back."

"Michael, thanks!" I wanted to clap my hands together but felt I'd better retain a little decorum. "I even have a horse to ride! Diane at Redwood Stables said I could ride him any time he was available. And we're going to plan a series of equestrian travel vacations with special meals and events and—"

"Okay, okay." He laughed. "We'll see how it goes."

I couldn't believe how excited I felt.

"What I'd like you to do is stay here for a month and work with Daniel. Then take a few weeks to go home, pack your things, and move out here."

Move out here. Wow! Yay! I'd be coming back to Redwood Cove and all the great people I'd met.

"Sounds good to me."

"See you tomorrow." Corrigan picked up his briefcase and left the room.

And he left me walking on clouds. I was valued and respected. I was part of a team. I had a new career. I had a new beginning. I'd found my place and my new home.

Please turn the page for an exciting sneak peek of

Janet Finsilver's next Redwood Cove Mystery

MURDER AT THE MANSION

coming in June 2016!

Chapter 1

A s I straightened out the Jeep after rounding a long curve, Red-wood Cove popped into view. White buildings, looking like small squares, dotted a grove of trees. The aquamarine Pacific Ocean crashed against rocky outcroppings on my left, spewing foam and creating swirling mists.

Redwood Cove. My new home.

Excitement pushed away the weariness of long driving hours from Wyoming. My heart beat faster and goose bumps rose on my arms.

"My new home." I whispered it aloud.

"My new job." I spoke it aloud.

Tiredness slipped away as my mind raced ahead. I kept my foot steady on the gas pedal, remembering the horse trailer I pulled behind me filled with my belongings. I turned off the song *Walking on Sunshine* playing on the radio, put the window down, and let the salty breath of the ocean pour in.

I visualized the business cards nestled in a leather case in my purse. "Resorts International" in raised letters at the top. "Kelly Jackson, manager, Redwood Cove Bed-and-Breakfast" artfully displayed in the middle. The cards would rest on the engraved brass holder my boss, Michael Corrigan, had sent me as a welcoming gift.

I turned off the highway and saw the steeple of Redwood Cove Bed-and-Breakfast standing out against the sky. As I pulled into the driveway of the B&B, I inhaled deeply, struck by the sheer beauty of the place as well as the intense sweet fragrance permeating the air. The brilliant array of flowers on the trellised vines created a kaleidoscope of color next to the elegant white sculpted pillars. Gingerbread trim adorned the two-story inn.

I drove to the back and pulled off to the side of the parking area by the garage. The back door of the inn burst open, and a ten-year-old boy bounded down the stairs followed by a short, heavy-set basset hound.

"Miss Kelly! Miss Kelly! Hi!" Tommy slid to a stop in front of me. "Welcome back." His tricolored hound, Fred, jumped up and down next to him, or at least as best he could. His upper torso could only clear the ground by a couple of inches.

I smiled. "Glad to be here, Tommy."

He flew by me with Fred at his heels and clambered up onto the fender of the trailer. "Did you bring a horse? Did you? Did you?"

"No, sorry Tommy. It's filled with my things."

Helen, Tommy's mother, had followed him outside. She wiped her hands on her apron and gave me a hug. "It's so good to have you back, Kelly."

I returned the embrace. She looked much better than the last time I saw her, with more color in her face and no longer gaunt and haggard looking.

"And it's wonderful to see you, Helen. And Tommy and Fred, of course." I smiled at her. "I'm excited to hear how things are going."

"Why the horse trailer?"

"I decided this trailer was the easiest way for me to haul my stuff. My parents are going to come for a visit in a couple of months when the weather at the ranch in Wyoming makes California sound good. They'll take it back with them then."

Tommy climbed down and patted Fred, who'd been unsuccessful at jumping up onto the trailer.

"I didn't bring a horse, Tommy, but I do have my saddle. Would you like to see it?" The last time I'd been here, Diane at Redwood Cove Stable had offered to let me ride an Appaloosa, Nezi, when the horse was available. I intended to take her up on it.

"You bet."

I went over to the trailer, unlatched the tailgate, and placed it on the ground, forming a ramp. The saddle was on a wooden stand I'd secured to the wall. Tommy rushed into the trailer and began to trace the intricate tooled leather pattern with his fingers.

"I'll be doing some riding at a local stable," I told him. "It's nice to have my own saddle because the stirrups are adjusted for me and the seat fits." *And it's part of my family life I'd brought with me.*

"Cool. Did you bring your bridle?"

"No, the bits used on the bridles are specific to each horse's needs. There are lots of different types."

Tommy reached out and touched my leather belt with the gold and silver championship barrel racing buckle. "Wow." His eyes were wide.

I had never heard a one-syllable word sound so long as when Tommy uttered that word. I had wrapped the belt around the saddle horn at the last minute. It wasn't everyday wear, but I'd ridden with it for years and decided to bring it along.

Before I could explain, my attention was drawn away to the rattling engine of an approaching vehicle. I looked down the driveway and saw a faded blue Volkswagen bus approaching.

I knew it well.

The vehicle parked at the back of the inn and tall, lanky Daniel Stevens emerged, the newly appointed manager of Ridley House, a sister property. His daughter, Allie, appeared from around the back of the bus. They were father-daughter look-alikes with their straight blue-black hair, high cheekbones, and copper-hued skin.

Daniel gave me a quick, friendly hug. "It's good to have you back."

"I'm glad to be here."

Allie smiled. "Hi, Kelly."

Tommy called out, "Allie, come look at this cool saddle and belt." She left to join him.

"How are the renovations coming?" I asked.

"Fine. They're on schedule," Daniel replied. "Should be done by the end of next week, and Redwood Cove B&B will be ready to open."

"Michael asked me to do an inventory of some historic items at a place called Redwood Heights and help out with a festival this weekend."

"He told me," Daniel said. "After acquiring Ridley House a couple of months ago, Michael decided to put Redwood Heights up for sale. It's a little different from his other properties," Daniel said.

A glance passed between Helen and Daniel.

I wondered what that was about.

"I've been helping with some repairs to get the place ready to sell," Daniel continued. "Michael's got an interested buyer. It's worked out well since I've been overseeing the construction on all three places."

Helen chimed in. "I've been preparing the afternoon appetizers. Since I was available, it made sense to give the cook at the Heights a chance to have a vacation."

"What's the event this weekend?" I asked. "Michael said you'd fill me in."

"The whales migrate this time of year," Helen explained. "And there's some great whale watching opportunities. Communities up and down the coast host various activities."

"What fun!"

"We call our festival Whale Frolic," Helen added. "There'll be a chowder contest and inns around town will have wine and gourmet treats for people to enjoy. Redwood Heights will be one of the places participating. The money from the tickets benefits the local hospital."

Daniel watched the kids happily chattering as they examined the saddle and the belt. "There's a social hour at five at Redwood Heights if you'd like to go tonight," he said. "That is, if you're not too tired."

"Sounds great. After all the sitting I've been doing, I'd enjoy some activity."

"We can introduce you to the manager, Margaret Hensley." He shot Helen another quick look.

What was going on between these two?

A creaking noise caused the three of us to look down the drive-way. A large motor home was crawling toward us, rocking gently from side to side. It drove by and parked in front of my Jeep.

Pictures of two larger-than-life beagles covered the side of the RV. One of them wore a pink collar, the other one blue. The slogan emblazoned next to them read, "Bedbugs? Termites? If you've got 'em, they'll find 'em. Call on Jack and Jill. Get the four-legged pros on the job and have a restful sleep tonight." A phone number was underneath it.

"Daniel?" I turned and looked up at him. "Is there something you haven't told me?"

Little did I know bedbugs and termites would be the least of my concerns in the coming days . . .

CPSIA information can be obtained
at www.ICGtesting.com
Printed in the USA
LVOW08s1506230117

521874LV00001B/229/P